**The German Town Of Heidelberg Is
About To Be Turned Upside Down.
Someone Is After Photojournalist
Brandon Noble And They Want Him Dead.
He Doesn't Know Why,
But He's Going To Find Out...
If It Kills Him.**

I WANDERED into the drawing room and there sat the beautiful girl I saw in the photograph. Her head was down now, her hands folded neatly in her lap. She looked up—I froze—she was an absolutely stunning goddess. My eyes were rivited to her as she rose to meet me.

"I'm with *Die-Bild-Zeitung*," I said. "Sorry to hear about your father." I didn't know what to say, but stumbled on, "I'm sure the police will find him in good health."

"You're American aren't you?"

"Yes ma'am, I'm on an exchange program—from New York—a parent company owns both our papers."

"Someone from the paper has already been here—"

"I'm a photojournalist; they write the story, I take the pictures."

"I see."

I marveled at her posture, at her tall sleek body wrapped in a burgundy silk ankle-length evening dress that clung to that exquisite form. She had succulent, pink lips that complimented long reddish-brown hair— hair that draped lazily over bare white shoulders.

"So you don't ask questions?"

PRAISE FOR ERIKA

"A campy cross between a Raymond Chandler
detective mystery and the sci-fi of
Karle Capek's R.U.R."
— Richard Kimberly, New York Herald

"A dark comedy that doesn't take itself
too seriously."
— J. Moon, Kansas City Beacon

Crammed full of classic European car chases,
knockdown fights, electrified trains, and a
beautiful and mysterious women."
— Martin Milner, Great Falls Chronicle

"A dark tale which gleefully employs beautiful
women, dungeons, mad scientists, and
a terribly mixed up detective."
— Paul Overstreet, North Boston Tribune

"A detective story that marches to its own
drummer...marching through many deft
descriptions of contemporary Europe and
ending in a surprising and dark climax."
— Marilyn Talbert, Kansas City Sun Times

"The final dénouement is a deliciously dark delight."
— Carey Lassiter, Westmont Daily Sun

ERIKA

By
Don Kirk

SWEETWATER STAGELINES™
SAN ANTONIO, TEXAS

ERIKA
© 2002, 2007 by Don Kirk
All rights reserved
including the right of reproduction
in whole or in part in any form

Published by
Sweetwater Stagelines™
an imprint of
The Old West Company™
5118 Village Trail Drive
San Antonio, Texas 78218

TRADEPAPER EDITION
ISBN-10: 0-9654341-3-3
ISBN-13: 978-0-9654341-3-3
Printed and bound in the United States of America

STORY SUMMARY:
A photojournalist stumbles on a sinister plot in
Germany that takes him into the lives of four
world-renowned scientists and a very unusual woman.

Detective Mystery, Science Fiction
Based on a 1973 screenplay outline by Don Kirk
Reviewed by Richard Kirschenbaum
Cover photos by Don Kirk

For information regarding special discounts for bulk
purchasers please contact the publisher at (210) 646-0227.
Single copies available at lulu.com/sweetwater

ERIKA

dedication

This book is dedicated to my father, Samuel Keith Kirk, who always wanted to try his hand at writing fiction, but never got around to it.

The Story of
ERIKA

As Told by Brandon Noble

WHAT Brandon Noble is about to tell you is a true story. It may seem fantastic to you at first. It's equally possible you will shuck it off—reject it as untrue. But please listen carefully and stay with him to the very end of his story. It is important that you are aware of the horror that has been going on behind your back. It is here among us all—right now, for us all to see, if it were not for the blinders we wear. In the 1970's, Brandon Noble tried to throw off his blinders and accept what was real: a horrible truth he dared to face and eventually succumbed to. The story is true as far as it can be reconstructed, based on the notes of an obsessed man and the newspaper stories, police reports, and videotape evidence that still reside in the Berlin National Archives. So heed, dear reader, what Noble is about to tell you, and never fall back on your staunchest beliefs or become apathetic to the things occurring around you.

Here then, is Noble's story:

one

DAY ONE. **Tuesday, April 1st.** It was the spring of 1973 and the weather was mild and perfect for an afternoon drive along the Rhine River—a river that meanders through a deep rocky gorge where wooded hills rise steeply on each side except where jagged rock is terraced for growing grapes for wine. At the water's edge—squeezed between river and hill—are the winegrower's villages built of picturesque half-timbered houses with tall gabled roofs. Perched on every rock projection is a medieval castle towering over the river, commanding the lush green valley in both directions. Tourists from around the world—and Europeans "On Holiday"—take romantic boat cruises lazily along the serpentine river as barges pass in both directions, day and night, carrying industrial goods to much of western Europe. The river passes through four countries and skirts a fifth, France. And all along the eight hundred miles of river, every castle, every island, every rock has a tale to tell—legends of chivalry and honor and lost love.

As I drove leisurely along the banks of the river, I contemplated this place and my place in it. Could I find peace here? Could I find love?

One of the most romantic areas of Germany, the Rhine and Nectar valleys speak of centuries of harsh history. It's beautiful architecture and craft industries—like glass blowing, wood carving, and clock making—have survived relentless battles among the Lords of the repressive feudal system of the Middle Ages—

I was coming back from an assignment in Koblenz, on my way to Heidelberg, a beautiful German city just twenty clicks East of Mannheim up the Neckar River Valley—

Old Heidelberg is nestled on the south bank of the Neckar and the ruin of Schloss Heidelberg stands majestically on a hill over the old medieval town. It still dominates the skyline, a testament to the power and influence it once had. Between huge guard towers stands what remains of the Great Hall with rows of windows four stories high, but through some of those windows, is the deep-blue April sky—

I pulled up onto the sidewalk in my weather-faded white VW beetle, the two driver-side wheels sitting on the sidewalk. There wasn't enough room to park a car on the narrow, cobblestone streets of old Heidelberg so this maneuver was quite legal. In only this way could another car pass. Three- and four-storied buildings towered as little as twenty feet across from each other creating a cozy human space, a space designed for people and not automobiles, laid out long before motorized vehicles were invented. Quaint little business signs hang over the sidewalk, their graphic lettering and scrollwork making them most attractive.

Using my latchkey, I entered the street door to my apartment building and climbed the steep narrow stairs to my one-room apartment. The kitchen was at one end of the room and the bed—a Murphy-style twin—could be pulled down from a wall cabinet. During the day, the room was my living and dining area. I used a folding TV-dinner tray to eat on while I watched the news on my nine-inch black & white set. A steam radiator set under the window, gurgling and popping a percussionists's tune on these cool spring days. The bathroom was down the hall in a tiny room not much bigger than the claw-foot bathtub standing within. A strange, gas-fired, hot-water-on-demand contraption hung on the wall above the tub. It didn't heat the water until you were ready to use it; the pilot light became a raging fire and heated the water as it rushed through a long coil of copper tubing. The *Toilette* was even further down the hall in another room, or shall I say closet—the Water Closet, known simply as the "WC". The toilet stood on a raised platform to provide room for a closet bend because the building didn't have plumbing originally. And worse: when the door was closed, your knees pressed up against the door. Just try standing up and pulling up your pants, it just wasn't possible; you had to open the hall door to do that. My apartment was small too, but comfortable. The price helped make it so.

I had been here for two months—and two years, but I didn't tell anyone that; I just told them I was over here from the states, temporarily assigned to *die Bild-Zeitung*, the newspaper with the big, bold headlines, exclusive photos, and lots of juicy gossip. It was Germany's most read newspaper though I think the readers liked the pictures even more than the stories. I made myself a sandwich with a few slices of *Bratwurst* and brown mustard, flipped on the TV, kicked off my shoes, and took a seat on my tattered couch. It was time for the evening news, something I tried not to miss, not just for the news, but for its entertainment value. I relished watching the news anchors flubbing their lines and trying to recover as they read the hand-written, paper-roll-type tele-prompters. And the stories, the human-interest stories, they were often just plain screwball: like the band of wild kittens on the loose that attacked laying hens in the town's barn-yards, the police unable to find their daytime "hideout." And the concrete lid on a septic tank that broke unexpectedly and a man fell in and drowned in the stinking sludge, his life coming to an end quite abruptly. I could only imagine what he took in with his last breath. And then there was the story of a thief without legs who robbed a clothing store and stole, among other things, eleven pairs of pants! What was he thinking? I couldn't imagine. And what crazy news I didn't get from German TV, I got from the welcome and reassuring, Armed Forces Radio Network—mainly because it was in English. My German wasn't that great—

The newscast was interrupted by a special report: *"Professor Wilhelm Wagner, the noted German biochemist and physicist has been kidnapped from his home in Schwetzingen. A witness said three men in a black Mercedes-Benz dragged the Professor from his home."* Photos of Wagner blanketed the screen and live video scanned his opulent mansion. The witness ranted on about the terrible, uncalled-for treatment the professor had received, but he was probably embellishing his story in the light of his new-found notoriety.

I leaned forward, watching intently. After a long moment, I grabbed my coat and camera, and scampered out the door. I wound my way through the serpentine streets of Old Heidelberg and drove into a parking lot accessed through a narrow archway—a parking lot that was once a farmer's barnyard.

Few lights were on, the news day apparently uneventful other than the kidnapping. The day shift had just left; those still there were finalizing the stories for the next morning's edition. The Wagner kidnapping would surely be the big story for tomorrow. Some of the reporters would be out running down leads, but me, I had a hunch of my own. I pulled open a file drawer among a long row of battleship-gray steel filing cabinets. Flipping through the files in the "S" cabinet, I found a file labeled "SUNSTONE LABORATORIES." News clippings and 8 x 10's stuffed the ragged folder. And here was what I was looking for: a photo of four men posing in front of a two-story black, brushed steel, post-modern glass-encased building with gold mirrored glass, quite out-of-place in an old city. One of the men was Wagner, the kidnapped scientist in the news report. The cutline read: *Professor Wilhelm Wagner, a renowned physicist, has, along with three colleagues, published a new theory on the relationship of matter to electrons. He plans to reveal what he calls an earth shak-*

ing experimental prototype at the Sunstone Laboratories next week. The photo was dated May 16, 1965. I flipped on down through the photos. One was of the two-story glass building engulfed in flames. I turned over the photo and found, taped to the back, a piece of paper with a file number and the cutline: *Last Night Sunstone Laboratories Exploded in Flames. No one Reported Injured, May 21, 1965.*

two

I HAD DRIVEN out to Schwetzingen, now pretty much just a suburb of Heidelberg—crammed with rows and rows of modern cinder-block residences—and crawled through the iron gates of the Wagner mansion, an elegant eclectic Gothic, quite formal in design, with Doric columns across the front. Scattered on the front drive, like a handful of discarded jellybeans, were dark-blue Volkswagen Beetles each with a flashing-blue, bubble-gum machine on the roof. A spotlight was strapped on the hood of each and a string of sirens was bolted across the front bumper. The insignia on the door panel read: *Heidelberg Polizei.*

No one stopped me as I entered the front door, my camera hanging neatly over my shoulder. Rich, wood paneling circled the foyer and a grand staircase rose elegantly to the second floor. I followed the action to a separate building at the back of the house where uniformed cops swarmed like black flies on roadkill.

"Sergeant, get this man out of here," barked the cop in charge upon seeing my face. He smiled as he barked, a deliberate technique, I think, to rattle me and keep me off balance.

"Inspector, you know I've got a job to do."

"What are you here for anyway, *Herr* Noble?"

"To get some photos."

"No, I mean over here in *Deutschland*?"

"I'm a Global Exchange Delegate at the paper."

"I know that, why you here in Germany?"

"We reporters trade places from time to time…to gain a new perspective."

"No, Mr. Noble, you skirt my question. You probably can go any country you want to and gain 'new perspective', as you say."

"I like Germany. Did my army tour of duty here…instead of in Vietnam."

"Lucky you, you must like the beer then?"

"I do…and the girls."

"The girls! Their unshaven armpits, ah, and their hairy legs, bah! Your American women far better looking than ours—but don't tell my wife I said so."

"I swear I won't."

"Then you can stay on my good side a little longer, but watch yourself, I haven't figured you out yet, *Herr* Noble."

Gerhard Schultz turned away, but then craned his head back to me, "You got any 'new perspectives' yet?"

"On the news?"

"*Ja*, the news, or *Deutschland*, or life in general, what else? That's what you do, no? Put perspective on screwed-up world."

"I just report the news…the true and indisputable facts."

"I'm sure it depends on who's telling it," said Schultz. "*Die Bild* is good with the facts."

"You noticed."—I changed the subject—"You got any clues on this case yet, Inspector?"

"That's for me to know—but I guess you find out. You been here for five minutes and already you're pain in my hemorrhoids."

"Just doing my job—I want to make a good impression, show my German comrades how it's done."

"How what's done? How bury rose thorn up Inspector's ass…"

"Inspector," interrupted one of the crime scene investigators, "take a look at this."

The Inspector turned his attention to the forensic specialist. I was surprised that I hadn't yet been asked to leave the premises, but the Inspector, Gerhard Schultz, was a good and patient man and I had dealings with him before: I bailed him out of a jam just two weeks earlier, passed along some information that allowed him to close a case. He knew he owed me and I knew I could call in that debt.

The Inspector was neatly dressed in his gray, woolen uniform with large white Lieutenant's bars on his lapels. Along with the standard service cap with its black visor and white felt top, he also wore a pair of orange shades—dark glasses that were just transparent enough to let you see his eyes. You didn't try to deceive those eyes, because somehow those glasses seemed to give the inspector the power to reach into your brain and gull you into telling the truth—assuming you knew the truth, and who of us does?

I meandered over to a long, black, marble-topped lab table, but I knew not to touch anything, I didn't dare. The room was filled with men attired in black jumpsuits who were dusting for fingerprints and taking photographs; the glare of flashbulbs blinding everyone like small nuclear blasts. One investigator pulled a measuring tape to size the room. Another flipped through a binder filled with perforated computer paper printed with thousands of lines of code. I wondered why they were examining this laboratory so closely? Why not examine the rest of the house or the driveway? Professor Wagner had been dragged from the house through the front door. They should dust the doorknobs, the telephone, the furniture, look for footprints, tire prints—

"*Herr* Noble! Don't touch anything."

"No, sir!" I wouldn't dare aggravate Inspector Schultz. I continued to take in the room: it was a crude laboratory with glass vessels, test tubes, a primitive microscope, slide rule, Bunsen burner, and even a small kiln. In a far corner sat an autoclave and a crude dynamometer for measuring foot-pounds of force. The place looked much like my high school physics lab, no particular field of science to be studied, just a sampling of many. Did the professor just dabble in science? The lab even reminded me of a back-alley electrical repair shop—one of those that repaired TV's and stereos and was cluttered with smoldering soldering irons, crooked shelves of dust-covered vacuum tubes, and oscilloscopes blipping incessantly with green sine waves. Also in Professor Wagner's lab, a stack of plain black tin boxes about four inches square with a toggle switch and voltage meter on them. What could he be working on? It was clearly a hodgepodge of equipment, but there had to be a common denominator.

I noticed ashes around the Bunsen burner and looked to the floor and saw a piece of computer paper that was burned at the edges where the tear-off line of holes were punched. I inched over to the paper and knelt down—and quicker than you can say "cheese", I'd picked up the paper and slid it into my coat pocket, so smoothly that I think I could've made a career as a pickpocket.

In the corner of the room was a built-in fireplace and on the mantle stood an ornate gold Victorian picture frame. I scooped it up and took a gander: a very pretty young woman graced the frame. Penned on the photo were the words: *To My Loving Father—Erika*. She was probably Wagner's daughter. I slipped on out of the lab and returned to the main house.

three

I WANDERED into the drawing room and there sat the beautiful girl I saw in the photogaph. Her head was down now, her hands folded neatly in her lap. She looked up—I froze—she was an absolutely stunning goddess. My eyes were rivited on her as she rose to meet me.

"I'm with *die Bild-Zeitung*," I said. "Sorry to hear about your father." I didn't know what to say, but stumbled on, "I'm sure the police will find him in good health."

"You're an American aren't you?"

"Yes ma'am, I'm on an exchange program—from New York—a parent company owns both our papers and they like to expand our education—and our travel—now that we're in a global media market."

"Someone from the paper has already been here—"

"I'm a photojournalist: they write the story, I take the pictures."

"I see."

I marveled at her posture, at her tall sleek body wrapped in a burgundy silk, ankle-length evening dress that clung to that exquisite form. She had succulent, pink lips that complimented long reddish-brown hair—hair that draped lazily over bare white shoulders. Her eyebrows curved delicately downward suggesting inverted crescent moons. Big chestnut eyes dominated her doll-like face.

"So you don't ask questions?"

That jolted me out of my trance, "Uh no, not usually, but could you…you see I have to identify the people in my photographs." Now was my chance, I reached for the 8 x 10 in my inside coat pocket and showed it to her. "These men, in this 1965 photograph, do you recognize any of them?"

"Yes, these are the men that worked with my father, Norman here, Montford…"

"Here, let me write these down."—I pulled a small, tattered notebook from my pocket—"My editor gets hopping mad when I get the names misspelled."

"Here on the left is my father, of course, Professor Wilhelm Wagner. W-A-G-N…"

"And the others?"

"Next is Dr. Norman Stuart, Dr. Montford Fouquet, and this is Dr. Boris Stravinsky."

"All doctors?"

"Dr. Stuart is the only one with a medical degree, the rest have University degrees."

"I see. Can you spell Stravinsky for me?"

"S-T-R-A-V…" Erika inched closer, peeking over at my scribblings and continued, "I-N-S-K-Y."

"Do you know where they live, or work, now?"

"Dr. Stuart lives in Heidelberg; Dr. Fouquet, I think, lives in Strasbourg."

"France?"

"Yes."

"How about Stravinsky?"

"I have no idea…you put all this on your photographs?"

"Well, the editor—in case we need to contact them for confirmation…of a story I mean…to verify information."

"I see."

"Yes ma'am. May I ask you where you were when your father was kidnapped?"

"You may ask."

"You didn't see him kidnapped?"

"No."

"Is there any reason you can think of why he might have been kidnapped? Arguments with co-workers…"

"Of course not. How dare you suggest such a thing!"

"I'm sorry, I didn't…all right then, well, thank you, I need to get some shots of the house out front if you don't mind."

"I'll have to ask my father. He's out…," Erica halted in mid sentence; Erika had, for a moment, apparently forgotten that her father was kidnapped.

"I'm sorry, they'll find him, *Fräulein* Wagner," I said as I made my way toward the front door. "Thank you, and don't worry, your father will be fine." I couldn't believe I had said that; I knew it was like a promise I had no right to make—and in no way could keep. I walked past the *Polizewagens* and turned back to snap a photo of the mansion with the Bug's parked randomly on the front driveway—looking like a ladybug convention. A glint of light hit my face. Out of the corner of my eye I could see a man with binoculars peeking above the stone perimeter wall.

I drove out the iron gate and flipped on the radio only to be greeted with another news bulletin: *Dr. Norman Stuart, noted scientist formerly with Sunstone, has announced that he intends to make an important public statement this afternoon.* Something was happening fast. Stewart would be the first I would go see.

four

2*56 Hauptstraße.* I pressed on the doorbell.

"Who is it?"

"I'm with *die Bild-Zeitung,* can I speak with you?"

After a long moment, the door buzzed; I quickly pushed

open the door before it could lock again. I bounded up several flights of stairs to the very top landing and found "*Zahl 7*" scratched on a wooden, three-panel door decorated with peeling paint. I knocked on it.

"Come in," answered a voice with an Australian accent.

I went in. A shaggy-haired man sat in a recliner, a gloomy expression on his face. He was in his sixties; his clothes were wrinkled and unwashed. He wore no shoes or socks on his feet. The apartment was small and plain, with little adornment. It was the apartment of a bachelor—a lot like mine—except this one-room apartment was in the attic level of a four-story building with rough-hewn collar beams and rafters penetrating the space just above my head. Cobwebs graced the highest corners of the room and a single dormer window lit the space—barely.

"Thank you Dr. Stuart. I won't take much of your…"

"Another reporter has already been here."

"From *die Bild-Zeitung*?"

"I think so."

"Oh, that scoundrel, those darn cut-throat cub reporters you know; always competing for the story. I apologize, sir, but maybe, since I'm already here, you could help me. I assume you've heard about the kidnapping of Professor Wagner?"

"Yes. What is it you want to know?" asked the Australian.

"I want to ask you about Sunstone Laboratories. You once worked there?"

Dr. Stuart slumped in his chair quietly, his dry wrinkled hands resting on the armrests. A bead of sweat ran out from under his white scruffy hair and dripped down his washboard forehead. He looked nervous and uneasy.

"Yes, I uh, did for a time."

"You're a medical doctor?"

"Neurologist, but I also have doctoral degrees in organic and electrochemistry."

"A chemist?"

"Brain chemistry; just theory and research."

"What exactly did you do at Sunstone?"

"Research."

"I understand that, but…"

"No you don't. Why are you here pestering me?"

"You're planning to make an important announce…"

"Not until this afternoon, and…and…"

"You're going public with something?"

"I am, and all you reporters can bloody well hear it at the same time…"

"Does it have anything to do with Sunstone?"

"This afternoon…"

"I'm sorry, but I must ask you about the explosion at the lab in 1965 that completely destroyed Sunstone?"

"Yes…it was destroyed." He shifted in his seat, nervous and impatient.

"Did they ever determine the cause of the explosion, spilled chemicals, a Bunsen burner maybe?"

"Uh yeah, a Bunsen burner I think it was, left overnight, that was it," replied Stuart quickly in a strained voice. He uncrossed and re-crossed his legs. "I need to get ready for my announcement, can you come back another time?" He started to stand up, but then dropped back into his cush-ioned recliner. His eyes had jutted past mine for a moment and I started to look behind me, but the doctor abruptly con-tinued, "What did you say your name was, young man?"

"Uh, Brandon Noble," I told him, and I had to repeat that I worked for *die Bild-Zeitung*. He said he didn't read it, just a lot of outlandish pictures. I didn't tell him I didn't read the darned thing either, but I thanked him for his time and left. He made no effort to escort me to the door. I closed the door behind me, left to tackle the eight flights of stairs— but at least they were *down*. But it's those turns after every flight—if you turn them too fast—that will make you dizzy, but that wasn't what was causing my head to spin, it was Dr. Norman Stuart. He was not at all relaxed. Something was wrong. He was nervous, sweating profusely and, in that poorly-insulated attic, it wasn't at all hot.

Something was terribly wrong. I had gone three flights when I turned around and bounded back up the stairs. I slammed my fragile, 150-pound body into the wood door, it cracked open splintering the doorframe. Inside was not what I wanted to see. I hurried to the kitchen and looked in. No one there. I peered into the bedroom: drawers open, clothes strewn about. I looked out the window; no one was running away in the street below. I turned back to Dr. Norman Stuart who lay there, on the floor, in a pool of bright-red blood, a piece of rusty barbed wire wrapped tightly, very tightly, around his pitiful neck.

I hopped into my little white Beetle just as a cop car drove up behind me. Two *Polizei* rushed past and pounded on the door buzzer labeled *"Zahl* 7." No one answered. I knew why. I eased off the curb hoping they hadn't noticed me and drove away.

five

DAY TWO. **Wednesday, April 2nd.** A high-speed electrified train zipped across the German landscape, past picturesque villages dating back hundreds of years, past farm fields and hay stacks and horse drawn wagons carrying huge loads of cow dung. I was on a Federal Republic inter-city train and glad the windows were closed.

The photograph of the four scientists lay on my lap. I was a newspaper photographer—or so I made it appear.

A camera was all that I needed, and sometimes I used a laminated press pass to hang around my neck to get access to restricted events. It was easy to make any press pass I needed, and a little acting and quick wit was all that was required to come off as a photojournalist. I knew people tended to trust what a stranger had to say, any stranger, anything he had to say. I didn't know why this was so, but I knew that's how the confidence man was able to take your money—well, he doesn't even have to take it, you *give* it to him voluntarily. He takes advantage of your good-heartedness, your unquestioning trust of a fellow human being. When the con artist finds a "mark" who *isn't* taken in by his sincere-sounding banter, you can bet he's found another man without scruples, another con man.

Dr. Norman Stuart seemed like a good man, but now he was no longer with the living, a loss to society I was sure, and he looked as if he had been lost for a very long time. He was a doctor, and yet he was living in squalor. How could this have happened?

I pulled out my pocket notebook and flipped it open to the names of the scientists Erika Wagner had given me: Stuart, Fouquet, and Stravinsky. I drew a line through Stuart's name.

An agricultural landscape zipped rapidly past the large picture window in my first-class rail car. I was the only one in a cabin containing two long bench seats that faced each other, each one long enough to sit three adults. The cabin door opened to a windowed-corridor that ran along one side of the train, but the door to my cabin was closed. The scream of the locomotive's whistle seared the air as we entered a tunnel. My cabin became dark; the lights flickered. After a few moments, bright sunlight blasted in again. The train was racing along the countryside, running at least eighty miles an hour, stopping traffic at road intersections for only a few seconds. A pedestrian had better not be on the track when a train was approaching—even if the train was several miles away: it was moving so fast and so quietly that it was easy for a person to be surprised by its sudden presence. A pedestrian could be smashed on the front of the locomotive like a bug on a windshield—and, like a car, the loco wouldn't miss a beat. The pedestrian would never know what had happened to him. He'd be there one minute, gone the next, like Dr. Norman Stuart. Life was fleeting, I knew that, but to see someone alive one minute—talking with him—then dead to this world the next; that was tough—on both of us.

He had been murdered so the other scientists could also be in danger. I was headed to France to see Dr. Fouquet, the next man on my list.

Scenery flashed quickly past my window, my reflection superimposed on the glass; I felt like I was riding an H.G. Wells's Time Machine. But I couldn't tell for sure. Were we going forward in time or backward? And where in Einstein's space-time continuum was home? When we were born, at age thirty, when? I was soon to be twenty-five and I didn't know where I was or who I was. How was I traveling relative to other passengers in the universe? Was I doing what I was put on this earth to do? Was I where I was supposed to be? The train gave me too much time for contemplation.

I marked an 'X' over the face of Stuart and returned the picture of the four scientists to a brown manila envelope. I pulled out today's *Bild-Zeitung* article reporting the Professor Wagner kidnapping. On the first page was a large photo of his mansion with Cop Beetles parked in the front driveway. It wasn't my photograph: my film was still in my camera.

In my brown envelope there was also the newspaper clipping about the explosion at Sunstone Laboratories. May 21, 1965—the building completely destroyed—destroyed just a few days *before* a new prototype was to be revealed. A new prototype? Of what? Years of research melted to nothingness. Here today gone tomorrow—

Also stuck deep within the envelope, was a small piece of computer paper burned at the edges. On it was part of a mathematical equation and part of what looked like an electrical schematic. What could it mean? Not the equation, I'd no chance with that. *Algebra I* was easy in high school, but *Algebra II* left me swinging in the wind, and the partial schematic of an electronic device, that was not my thing either. No, why had a piece of paper with an equation on it been *burned*? There were ashes around the Bunsen burner; maybe Professor Wagner was trying to burn it to keep the kidnappers from getting hold of it. Maybe they weren't after him, just what he had or what he knew. And if that were true, this equation might be important.

The landscape rushed by. Farmers plowed their fields, horse drawn wagons waited at rail crossings. The world was moving slowly and predictably out there while the train was zipping through it. A time machine? Definitely a different perspective. The train whistle screeched. I put everything back in the brown envelope and wrote boldly across its face the name "ERIKA." I placed the envelope in my overcoat which lay neatly beside me.

A sudden knock on the door, the conductor had come to punch tickets—or so I had assumed.

I reached to get the door handle, but before I could—

The door was flung open.

A large beefy, ape of a man squeezed through the narrow doorframe. He was dressed sloppily in a dark suit and off-center tie. A businessman? I didn't think so. The Paul Bunyon of Europe? Maybe.

The man stepped in, closed the door, deliberately locked it, and sat down across from me. He had a small black case hanging from his shoulder.

I sat there calmly, my eyes fixed on the burly man. He crossed his arms and grinned. I smiled back with strained effort. I had the uneasy feeling he wasn't just a passenger, he might have plans for little old me. He said nothing, just stared intently. I guess he thought his awesome girth would explain everything. It didn't.

"You're a big man," I said.

"You're cockroach under boot," he replied with a deep voice and broken accent.

"You sure I'm not sticky chewing gun you'll have a hard time leaving behind?"

He didn't reply, I don't think he understood.

"You're not German are you?" I continued.

He shook his head and then mumbled, "Slav."

"Slav, you're from Yugoslavia?"

He nodded his head and then added, "Belgrade."

"Ah, I see, nice city."

"You been there?"

"No," I replied.

He looked at me confused, trying unsuccessfully to process the information. I didn't want him to.

I continued, "What's your handle?"

"Handle?"

"Your name."

"Branko Tanovic."

"I like that name," I said. "Your mother must have liked you." The beetlehead had just given me his name. I decided to press him for more.

"How long have you been in Germany?"

"Four year."

"Pretty place huh? You like it here?"

He nodded and said, "Good beer."

It figured. I admit, the beer *was* good, but that wasn't what interested me about Germany.

Suddenly a sharp knock on the cabin door and we were brought back to our tenuous situation. The big lug dropped his crooked grin and turned fearful.

"Tickets," called a muffled voice from outside.

At that, the Slav's eyes left mine for a moment and I took the opportunity to jump up and throw one swift kick to his Paul Bunyon balls. He buckled over easily; his black case fell to the floor. I wasn't going to wait for him to return the favor so I calmly grabbed my overcoat, straightened my turtleneck sweater and tan tweed sport jacket, brushed my mussed hair, picked up *his* black case, and then casually opened the cabin door. I handed my ticket to the conductor and stepped past him out into the corridor.

Clip, clip, drove the ticket punch. The conductor returned my ticket and then noticed the beefy man bent over on the seat, his hands holding his crotch.

"He's sickened from the food—the food from your dining car. Bad Hungarian goulash, I think he said."

The conductor looked back at the pained man as I strolled down the corridor, putting on my overcoat.

six

I TRAVERSED the full length of the first-class passenger car and opened the door leading to the vestibule—that drafty space between cars with its loud, clacking track noises and whooshing air. The rock and roll of the cars made this an uncomfortable, but exhilarating place to ride.

I opened the Yugoslavian's black case and pulled out a pair of binoculars. This Slav had to be the spying man at the Wagner Mansion—

Suddenly, a dark image lunged toward me with a knife, a long knife—as big as an "Arkansas Toothpick". I deflected the knife with the binoculars: the neckstrap was cut and the binoculars crashed to the deck.

A short, stubby man—a repulsive looking, greasy-haired man with a rough, pock-marked complexion—brought the knife around and under my arms, going straight for my kidney. I grabbed his wrist and held back the wicked knife. I banged the knife against the wall. The ugly weasel lost his grip and the knife clanged to the steel floor.

He jabbed me in the stomach with his left fist, and then with his right, struck my face with a glancing blow. I tried to get my knee into the man's crotch, but the close quarters, the inability to get some real force behind the thrust, I was unable to do it. The man then grabbed me around the neck in an attempt to crush my windpipe.

I returned the favor by grabbing the little man around *his* neck with both my hands and then squeezed as hard as I could. He was standing up a step, which now put us face to face, eye to alarming eye. One man had to die. There was no other option. The vestibule was like a two-man coffin—we were wrapped in iron and steel—but one of us didn't intend to stay there. The runt's eyes were bugging out. My eyes were bulging and ready to pop. Sweat trickled from both our foreheads. Neither one of us could grunt a sound.

Flanged wheels squealed as the train hit a tight turn—

And we were thrown down the steps and against the closed vestibule door. We lost our grip on each other. The resolute weasel eyed his frog sticker on the floor and reached for it. His fingers scratched at it. He pulled away from me and grabbed up the knife, and in one swift move, slashed at me. The knife ripped through my overcoat—

—but caught in the lining.

I went with an uppercut to the jaw that separated him from his chin and I wondered where he would land. He hit the wall and went limp, falling onto the steps. I pulled myself from under the man and climbed over him. I opened the vestibule door—the ground streaking by outside, the track noises much louder now. The steel-truss towers that supported the overhead electric lines flashed by. I grabbed the unconscious man by the shirt and pulled up on him—

Just then I saw the big palooka towering over me—that Yugoslavian with the mean, unforgiving eyes—and aching crotch—

And I found myself tumbling through the air like a cowboy over the horns of a seething bull. I was helpless to do anything, my arms flailing, my body twisting, the whole world spinning out of control around me.

Mt parents will be furious, I thought, with venomous hatred for the man who took my life. They'd probably never know who the Slav was and never have the chance to be comforted by the knowledge that he would be put to death, an eye for an eye; isn't that what the Bible recommends. Me, I wasn't religious, I didn't know if there was a god, so I wasn't worried about dying, I was just saddened by my parent's sadness; I could see tears running down their faces. I was kicking myself for making a mistake; I had messed up and I was waiting for that past that was supposed to flash before my eyes. And where was that light at the end of the tunnel? I didn't see a light; I didn't see a tunnel. I didn't see anything. And then I began to focus on my body, my flesh and bones. How was I going to hit? Head first? How best to survive the fall? Maybe I should keep my arms to my chest. No, I should cover my head. No, I can't survive this! I'm going to be hit by a steel tower at eighty miles an hour. I'm waiting—any moment now—waiting to be forced through a web of steel like hamburger through a meat grinder—

Why now must I leave this earth? I had just met the most beautiful girl in Germany, maybe in the world, and I had lots more to do; I wasn't ready to go. I wasn't ready to die. What dying man is able to talk about his last moments? Well, I'll tell you the first thing he thinks about is how his family will be seething with anger for the man who took his life, be it with a knife, a gun, an automobile or, by being thrown from a speeding train.

seven

MY FLAILING body shot through a huge haystack and came out the other side—hay exploding outward. I hit the ground and rolled down a long hill. Rolling over and over, I eventually came to a stop.

I was still alive.

The train whistle screamed.

The Yugoslavian, Branko Tanovic, a buffoon of the lowest order, a dumb brute who worked for someone, I knew I'd see him again, and I'd be ready, I had his number, I knew his weakness. But why was he after *me?* A big man with binoculars, had he been watching me? Following me? Had I stumbled onto something big in my own stupid way? And was this the same man who strangled Dr. Stuart with a piece of barbed wire? The doctor's juggler penetrated with sharp wicked points, draining him of five quarts of blood in just a few gurgling moments. I could only guess he was killed because he was about to go public with something someone didn't want known.

My thoughts shifted to Erika. Her eyes were mesmerizing, windows to her exuberant spirit—gleaming with the wonder of a child's. She had looked directly at me, into my eyes, trying desperately to acquire information about me. She had been dressed to the nines. Her outfit fit perfectly, not a wrinkle, not a fold of cloth without skin to cover. She was perfection, like the laws of nature. Me, I was half-way-decent looking—Hollywood handsome actually, windblown sandy hair, the Robert Redford type—but did she see me that way? I could only hope.

Another train whistle screamed.

I opened my eyes.

A train flew past as quickly as thought, and became the size of a toy train in a flash.

I shook my head and stood up, brushed the hay from my coat, and straightened my ruffled hair, the image of Erika still on my mind.

I had been on my way to Dr. Fouquet's home and I still had that goal. He could be in danger. I looked down the long track as it ran to the horizon in both directions. It was quiet. The air felt crisp and cool. I was already in France and it couldn't be much farther to Strasbourg; I had only to follow the railroad right-of-way. I was moving much slower now that I was off the Time Machine. It was actually quite nice. There was time now to look around, watch the birds, smell the wild flowers, feel the ground underfoot, and taste the unique aroma of the French countryside: there were huge mounds of cow and pig dung everywhere. And on the ground below me, dung beetles struggled with balls of crap many times their own weight, pushing and tugging, trying to get somewhere. They reminded me of employees in corporate America, working their asses off and getting nowhere. I could hear the sound of a farm tractor puffing and snorting off in the distance. I could hear the calming clang of an iron bell ringing out the time in a distant clock tower. Time was indeed moving forward.

eight

A BUTLER in coattails met me at the door and after reporting my presence, led me across a pink marbled foyer walled with beautiful Flemish tapestry and tiled mosaics of very scary dragons. But it was the imposing knight that caught my attention: a full suit of shining armor for a sixteenth-century knight stood seven-foot tall on a small oak platform. A long sword held between his gloved hands, reached from his chest to his feet. Everything except the crooks of the arms and the back of the knees would be covered with very hard plates of steel.

I was brought into a game room where a well dressed, imposing man in ascot and smoking jacket bent over to line up a shot. His cue stick popped a white ball and it glided across a red-felted billiard table. It hit one cushion and then another and then hit the purple seven ball, deflecting it obliquely into a corner pocket.

"Doctor, this is *Monsieur* Noble of *die Bild-Zeitung; Monsieur* Noble, this is Doctor Fouquet."

"Thank you, André."

The butler turned on his heels and smartly left the room. The heavy-set black-haired billiard player, with neatly trimmed mustache, lined up another shot and with a few mental calculations, popped the cue ball gently, but firmly. It bounced off the foot cushion and then rolled slowly back and hit the red-striped eleven ball into the right center pocket.

"Nice shot!" I said.

"So what do you want to see me about, Mr. Noble?" asked the doctor, apparently irritated by my presence and squinting as if I was an unexpected ghostly vision. He re-chalked his fine mahogany cue stick.

"Dr. Fouquet, sir, I wonder if I could have a few moments of your time to talk about Sunstone Laboratories?"

"You American, no?"

"Yes sir, from Buffalo, New York," I replied.

"I own company there in States, two actually, large plastics manufacturing company and PLCS—Programmable Logic Control Systems."

"What does it do?"

"We build industrial computer systems that determine the timing and movement of machines within an assembly plant. We've a system at the Mercedes plant in Stuttgart."

"Ah, very good, sir. Have you heard, your old colleague Professor Wagner has been kidnapped?"

"No, can't say I have."

"He was taken from his home in Schwetzingen by three men."

"Good man, Wilhelm. I spend many pleasurable years working with him."

I walked over to a green-velvet wall decorated with antique medieval weapons. A large crossbow of wood and iron and an intimidating battle-axe hung neatly next to a mace, one of those spiked iron balls on a chain designed to give an enemy the most poignant of headaches. A Medieval coat of arms scrolled with the name "FOUQUET" graced the end wall along with framed diplomas in Applied Mechanics, Hydrodynamics, and Kinesiology.

"What is that Doctor, Kin-es-e-ology?"

"Study of muscular movements in humans," he replied.

"Interesting," I said, but his response didn't tell me much—and he knew it didn't and added:

"I study kinetic theory, motion of masses in relation to forces acting on them."

"Great, that's very fascinating," I said.

"I also dabble in the new computer sciences—integrated circuits, silicon field-effect transistors, you taking notes?"

"Uh, no, I've a good memory," I replied. I was getting nowhere. I pointed to a framed photo on the wall, "Doctor, these four men in lab coats? I see you and Professor Wagner and…"

"Yes, men I once worked with."

"The four of you must have been very close."

"Yes, we spend many years together on some, you know, significant projects."

"What kinds of projects did you work on at Sunstone?"

"You know, we were innovators—inventors, basically—new medical technologies, hydraulic hospital beds, remote devices using laser technology, powered wheelchairs, that's all."

"I remember a wheelchair in *Popular Mechanics*, a quadriplegic could operate it with his chin. Was that yours?"

"Yes, as a matter of…"

"That was great, Doctor! No small accomplishment I'm sure."

"It's a team effort—lots of support, lots of money."

"I'm still impressed," I said.

"So, why interested in story now—just because Professor Wagner kidnapped? No! You not interested in my work, you want to find Wilhelm."

"I want to know what happened at Sunstone Laboratories, why the explosion that burnt the building to the ground?"

Dr. Fouquet bent over to take another shot, "Boris, he…"

"Boris Stravinsky?" I interrupted.

"Yes, Boris Stravinsky, he broke with us, not agree on direction we taking with project. The pressure, too much for him, I think. A good man, but he and company not see eye to eye."—Fouquet took his shot. The green, six-ball bounced off the curb, one, two, three times and dropped neatly into the intended corner pocket. His angles were perfect. Only one ball was left to play, the black eight ball.

"What were you working on?" I asked.

"I can't say, it's still in works, top secret you understand."

"I thought Sunstone Laboratories was no more?"

"It's my project now."

"I see, and you don't know how the fire started at Sunstone?"

"No, they never able to determine cause, but I think Boris had something to do with it."

"Boris?"

"Boris, bitter man." Fouquet calmly chose his next shot and took aim.

"Then sir, who killed Dr. Stuart?"

Fouquet's shot went awry: the cue ball missed the eight ball entirely. He straightened up slowly, looking perturbed and replied in a rather blasé manner: "He dead too? Such a *tragédie*; I can't believe it. You no think it coincidence?"

"No sir, I do not."

"Well, I know nothing of it. We haven't worked together for many years—our original, how you say, 'concept' abandoned long time ago."

"Sorry to hear it, it must have been a very special project, Doctor. I can't help but notice, you live in a fine home, sir, very fine indeed, but Dr. Stuart, he had lots of fine degrees too, but he lives—*lived* in a small attic apartment."

"I don't know what happen to the man, cognitive dissonance."

"Sir?"

"Lost touch with reality."

"I see...well, I won't bother you anymore; I've already messed up your game."

"You amuse me *Monsieur* Noble, like a good *comédie*... André...ANDRÉ! My manservant will show you out. He make good squire."

"I'm sure."

"I hope you enjoy visit to our country. *Bon soir.*"

I was escorted out quickly; I could only take in a morsel of his home: in the drawing room, I could see a beautiful four-foot statue of a Japanese Shogun standing at attention in a colorful silk robe. In his day, the Shogun was a military dictator, one who exercised absolute control over his dynasty and took power away from all the emperors of Japan. I felt like Dr. Fouquet was that kind of man: a control freak. And Fouquet had made a slip. Was he aware of it? He had said, "He dead *too*?" Does he know Professor Wagner to be dead? I hoped he wasn't—or so much for promises to the lovely Erika. And this secret project: he said the original project had been abandoned long ago and yet just moments before, he had said it was *his* project now. Hum, lies, I thought, will always get you caught.

nine

DAY THREE. **Thursday, April 3rd.** It was a given that I would want to see Erika again. I couldn't wrench her from my mind and I wasn't trying to. Even with all that was happening, her vision remained burned into my memory. Her beauty had kept me awake all night. I had felt a tingle that I couldn't throw off, and today, I had a legitimate reason to call on her. I rounded a bend in my Volkswagen—a Volkswagen that was frayed around the edges but otherwise in good working order. I had bought it used, very used. The guy that sold it to me had bought it from a GI going home, and *that* GI had done the same. I was sure the speedometer had rolled past the 99,999 mark several times. This VW, built in the early 60's, was still cooking; it had just four cylinders and fifty-two cubes, but it got me where I wanted to go. And right now, that was Erika's.

I pulled up to a huge black wrought-iron gate and pushed the intercom button.

"Yes?" cracked the com.

"It's Brandon Noble, the reporter, uh the photographer, from *die Bild-Zeitung.*" I looked into the passenger seat to see if my Nikon was there. It was.

"Yes, Mr. Noble?"

"I really need to talk to you again."

"The picture of our home in your paper was nice," she replied, "it was on the *front* page!"

"Yes, they liked it. All those funny looking police cars."

"Like a bunch of jelly beans."

"Yeah, like that."

"Well please, come in."

The iron-gate squeaked open slowly as if daring me to enter. I drove on up the circular drive and stopped in front of a two-story residence with a steep, grey slate-roof with a prominent entrance: wide double doors in an exotic wood maybe ten feet tall and carved with mystical figures. It was the first time I had noticed these doors, I guess because they had been fully open on my first visit. The doors sat in the midst of a huge pointed archway of dark stone with a god-awful-looking creature staring down at me: bulging eyes, gritted teeth, huge dog-like ears. What kind of man could dream up such fantastically grotesque creatures? Had he had a bad trip on drugs when he sculpted it? No doubt. It would definitely scare away the evil spirits—and even some of us not so evil.

One of the huge doors creaked open.

"Good day, Mr. Noble—is that it?"

"Yes. You can call me Brandon."

"Come in, Brandon. Is that German?"

"What? Oh, Brandon. It's Celtic, means 'prince', but it's a British derivation—from St. Brendon who discovered the New World."

"I see, I thought Columbus discovered America?"

"History is always being re-written."

"*Ish sehen.*"

Erika led me into the drawing room. She walked so perfectly, carefully placing one foot directly in front of the other. She wore high heels in a world where everyone else was beginning to wear tennis shoes. Her nails were perfectly manicured. She led me to a nice burgundy leather chair. She looked so very metropolitan in her white blouse with a bow collar and gray sheath dress that stopped well below the knees. The dress fit snuggly to her splendidly sculpted curves, the fabric pulling divinely around her hips.

"Were you just going out?" I asked, "I didn't mean to interrupt you."

"Oh no, Mr. Noble. I was just doing a little cleaning up."

Uh-huh, I thought, in *that* getup. "You're cleaning up to keep your mind off your father…"

"Yes, I think so."

"You speak very good English. Your father is German?"

"Yes."

"*Fraülein* Wagner, may I call you Erika?"

"Yes, Mr. Noble, you may."

"And you may call me Brandon."

"Fine."

"Erika, to get to the point: I wonder if we could go somewhere and talk. Could I take you to a neighborehood café? It's close to lunch time."

"*Ich sehen.*"

"Pardon me I don't—what did you say?"

"I see."

"See what?"

"I understand, you want to take me to lunch."

"That's right. So may I?"

"Fine."

"If that means 'yes', grab your coat and lets go."

"Fine."

'Fine' must be her favorite word, I thought, as she uncrossed her slender legs, rose from her chair, and sashayed out of the room. A gorgeous woman she was—definitely. But I was a bit confused, she seemed a little slow on the uptake. But then again, maybe she just didn't understand English that well, or maybe she was lost in her thoughts, worried about her father. Sure that must be it. The trip to the café might get her mind off the kidnapping—and maybe on me. I hoped.

ten

WE SAT in a corner café where we could see out the window and up and down the little cobblestone streets, watching people walking, talking, and shopping. We watched the bustle of small cars, Mercedes-Benz delivery trucks, and horse-drawn lorries as they wound their way through the narrow streets of Schwetzingen. Shops were on the street level and the owners lived above them. And along any street, behind double doors, you could find a barnyard—in the middle of town. The milk cows were stabled at ground level so that in winter their rising body heat would provide warmth for the family living upstairs. The city ordinance writers of America would go berserk. A person can bicycle to work or hop a quiet electrified tram between picturesque villages—villages separated by farm fields, forests, and green hills—not at all like the urban sprawl of America's single-family homes. The green trams charged through the streets on narrow tracks imbedded in the cobblestones, a band of tinted windows circling the top half of the vehicle, and plastered along the bottom: colorful advertising cards. A trolly pole protruded above each caterpillar like an insect antennae, there to lick at the life-giving electricity. But I digress. The café was cozy, quiet, and laid back. Guests were encouraged to stay as long as they pleased, play checkers, talk, guzzle beer, and guzzle more beer—good German *bier*—and every village had it's own home-grown brew. It was a great country for beer coaster collectors. I had started a collection of my own.

I gulped down a tankard of *Heineken*, a good Dutch lager. And maybe I'd have another. But Erika was sipping quietly on a cup of hot tea. Sitting there quite formally, she didn't put her elbows on the table and she didn't slouch. Maybe she was enjoying herself; I wasn't quite sure.

"Can I order you something to eat?" I asked.

"Maybe some *fritters*...but no, I think not, this will be fine."

"I was hoping to order myself a good *Weiner Schnitzel*, but I can't gorge myself while you just watch."

"*Weiner Schnitzel,* a Viennese cutlet! Is that the best you can come up with? Such simple tastes for interesting man."

"Well, I'm American, what do you ex..."

"May I suggest a *Cordon Bleu*. It too, is a veal chop, but with sliced ham and Swiss cheese all rolled together and dipped in eggs and bread crumbs and then fried to a beautiful golden brown."

"Are you out of breath?"

"No, should I be?"

"I think I satisfied my appetite just hearing your recipe."

"Fine."

"But I'll have a *Cordon Bleu* anyway. A suggestion from a lady as pretty as you has to be delicious." I had to get a compliment in somewhere and this was the best I could do. Well, she did call me interesting didn't she?

"*Fräulein! A Cordon Bleu für das Ehrenmann und noch ein bier, bitte.*"

"*Ja, Fräulein,*" the waitress replied and quickly retreated.

I smiled at Erika with a pleasing sense of excitement.

"I speak six languages," she said.

"Oh, really!"

"Once you learn the second one, the rest are easy."

"Where did you learn them?"

"Hum, at the University of Heidelberg, I think."

"You think?"

"I think."

"Good," I said. "It's good to think."

"Yes, it's good."

"Well, I was just thinking—with all those languages at your disposal—I wonder if you could help me find this Dr. Stravinsky? He might be able to help us find your father."

"You think he's fine?"

"I'm sure your father's all right," I said, immediately cursing myself. I'd repeated my first idiotic promise to her. "But Erika, I noticed there were no police at your home when I picked you up. You haven't received a demand for dough from the kidnappers?"

"Dough? For making bread?"

"No, money, a ransom note."

"I know not all your American slang. I'm sorry."

"Ah no, my fault."

"I'm sorry."

"No, no," I leaned forward and touched her precious little hand, "you're wonderful, *Perfecto!*"

"I have not received a demand for dough from the kidnappers," she replied.

"Well, that's a bit strange. Okay—well, after we eat—after I eat—what do you say we go find this Dr. Stravinsky?"

"I see."

"You do?"

"Yes."

"Okay then, lets do it."

eleven

ERIKA HELPED me make a few phone calls. It was one thing to try to ask a German on the street a few questions using a few *Berlitz* phrases and hand gyrations, but entirely another matter to communicate with a foreigner over a telephone line. Erika made that easy. There was not one single Stravinsky in the local phonebook. We thought we had a lead in the nearby town of *Karlsruhe*, but that didn't pan out either. We had the operator look up the name Stravinsky in the other major cities of southern Germany—*Düsseldorf, Cologne, Frankfurt, Stuttgart, Nuremberg,* and *München*—but still no Stravinsky turned up.

"Boris Stravinsky, that's a Russian name," Erika pointed out.

"Hum, maybe he lives up in Berlin," I added, "but that's a long shot."

"A what?"

"Oh sorry, more slang, means a slim likelihood of being successful. The odds of him being in Berlin just because the city is close to Russia, well…but it's a lead."

"A lead?"

"A lead's a…a direction like…here, we'll go to the library, they'll have the big city phone books."

“Okay.”
“Where’d you pick that one up?”
“What one?”
“The word ‘okay’.”
“From you.”
“Oh.”

Erika and I hopped a tram to the local *Bibliothek* and soon we netted us a Boris Stravinsky—several “Boris Stravin-skys,” in fact—in *Berlin* sure enough.
“You’ll get your man now, Mr. Noble.”
“What? Did you use…you did! That’s slang.”
“I’ve been *boning up* on your colloquialisms. They make for a more colorful speech.”
“They sure do. That’s great, but how did you pick up so many new…”
“I read a book of American slang here in the library.”
“Wow, I’m amazed! You’re good.”
“You can take that to the bank.”
“Oh no, I hope you haven’t gone off the deep end.”
“There, you used one too.”
“Erika, I’m taking you home. I’ll go to Berlin myself to check out Stravinsky.”
“Okay.”
‘Fine’ was not in her vocabulary anymore. I dropped Erika off at home and I was on my way to the *Bahnhof*.

It wasn’t long before the train pulled into the multi-tracked Berlin rail station, a large, bustling, and confounding station to us foreigners. A destination board as big as the side of a barn had hundreds of stations listed on it, and crowds of hurried travelers scurried in every direction. Rays of light from thousands of panes of glass penetrated the thick, grimy air. I just wanted to find the way out…to daylight.
Finally outside, I found the sky was cast in a dreary gray,

in fact, even the buildings were brushed with a gloomy gray and dull brown pallet of colors—no warm reds or cool greens to be seen anywhere and a thick, choking haze hung over the town. This wasn't Heidelberg.

I had several addresses to find so I bought a city map and hopped onto the blue *Stadtrundfahrten* double-decker bus—this one would eventually circle back to where I got on, reducing my chances of getting lost in this metropolis.

I climbed the circular stair to the top deck. It was a fun place to ride and enjoy the city—its architecture and its people—but I had to keep one finger on the map, watching for the names of every street intersection. A missed street and I'd have a tough time figuring out where I was. We passed a huge pile of stone rubble on the *Kurfürstendamm*, the city's main drag. It was a church left there in ruins as a reminder of the horrible destruction caused by the war. Two modern polygonal glass buildings, shaped like a lipstick case and powder compact, flanked the ruins and served as the new church and bell tower. The rest of West Berlin had been completely rebuilt so little of the old Berlin remained. All over the city, workers were laying and re-laying the cobblestone streets. It was one way that the socialist Germany kept everyone employed. We passed a huge, two-story-high, hand-painted movie poster advertising *Brankous ünd Alexandra* with Laurence Oliver, the epic story of the Russian revolution. I didn't figure that revolution was going so well. The bus then ran along the Berlin Wall separating the East from the West, parts of it just the brick fronts of abandoned buildings, windows still in place, some still with curtains, but behind them, a two-foot thick brick wall. And behind that, a no-man's zone—a kill zone—with tank traps, concertina wire, and foreboding guard towers with sullen soldiers— never a smile on their faces—their duty to watch for, and shoot down, any refugees trying to leave East Berlin. With their crow's-nest view of the West—a West teeming with life and lively commerce completely contrary to the East's—is it any wonder that the other assigned duty of these border guards was to watch for fellow guards trying to run the gauntlet to freedom. Barbed wire memorials with flowers and wreaths were set up along the sidewalk to denote the places where East Germans had attempted to breach the wall and escape—and didn't make it.

We passed Check Point Charlie, the bridge from the American sector of Berlin to the Communist East. Russian and American soldiers stood at opposite ends standing guard with loaded rifles. A white foreboding plywood sign printed in three languages—Russian, German and English—read: YOU ARE LEAVING THE AMERICAN SECTOR. I had once been across that bridge, through two checkpoints and back again—a sobering trip—and while I was over there, I didn't know whether I would ever be allowed to return. Over there the Russians appeared lifeless. Clothed in drab coats and gray scarves, they passed each other without acknowledging the other's existance and displayed no normal human facial expressions. They appeared to be very unhappy beings. The buildings were still in ruins, shrapnel scarring the few surviving facades. An exclusive retailer had in its display window, a white 1920's claw-foot bathtub and a stack of real bars of soap. Who knows what they sold for: a year's wages, maybe more. And Russians had to stand in line for hours to get a roll of toilet paper, paper that felt more like sandpaper than tissue. On this day, thankfully, I didn't have to go to the East—

I rang the bell on a gated door; everyone had gates on their doors.

A large lady with a massive black hairdo and white apron came to the door. I showed her a picture of Stravinsky, but she exhibited no sign of recognition. So it was off to the next address.

"Nein, Herr, Ich weiss nicht das Mann," and the door was

closed in my face. I was feeling like a gumshoe who was loosing his soul.

The third address I couldn't find. I was on the right street, in the right block—I thought—but there was a *"327,"* a *"329,"* and over on the other side a *"328."* But I needed a *"327-1/2."* I stopped an old woman lumbering along the cobblestones with a gallon bucket in each hand, each bucket full of something that made me want to puke, curdled milk maybe, bedpan cleanup, afterbirth, I didn't want to know. I showed her the picture of Stravinsky. She nodded in recognition—I couldn't believe it—and then pointed down a narrow alleyway.

I rambled down the back alley looking for the house number. The alleyway was barely wide enough for the smallest of vehicles. Battered milk cans sat outside the small doorways and trash cans of innumerable designs littered the street. I passed a large man wrapped in a bloody apron as he poured a wooden bucket of bright-red blood into the gutter. He must have come out of a restaurant—or a slaughterhouse.

Finally, there it was *327-1/2 Rückstraße.* I stepped down two stone steps into a covered entryway and knocked on the small door.

"Guten Morgen!" I said with forced enthusiasm; I was growing tired—and my feet hurt.

A slovenly, unshaven man wearing overalls and smelling of cow dung answered: *"Ja?"*

"Are you Dr. Boris Stravinsky?"

The man looked at me strangely; he apparently hadn't heard that "Doctor" salutation in a long time.

"Kommen innerhalb," he said and motioned me in.

Stravinsky led me into his little kitchen; it was painted a putrid baby-crap yellow—the walls, the cabinets, everything. The sink was full of dirty dishes. He sat down at a cockeyed breakfast table on which sat an overflowing ashtray and a half-empty beer. He placed his elbows on the table and gulped a big, long swig of his brew.

"*Nehmen Sie Platz*—please, sit!"

"Thank you, sir."

"*Was wünschen Sie?*" he asked.

I wish for you to take a bath, I thought to myself, but instead said, "I need your help. Your colleagues are in trouble down in Heidelberg."

"My *colleagues*? They screw me in the ass, why should I care?"

"Professor Wagner is missing—kidnapped actually, and Dr. Stuart is dead. He was murdered."

"Screw them, screw them all."

"What happened at Sunstone?"

Stravinsky took another drink and finished off the bottle. He reached over to the small round-topped, 1950's GE refrigerator and reached in for another beer.

"Care for one?"

"Don't mind if I do," I said—my mouth was dry. There was a good time for a beer, and this was one those times. Not because I was thirsty from traipsing through the streets of Berlin, but because I might be able to break a little ice, get Stravinsky to talking. I popped the top with a bottle opener and took a swig. "That hits the spot."

"You're too young to be drinking, it's bad habit to start."

"Everyone drinks here in Germany."

"And everyone got liver trouble."

"What do you do these days, Doctor?"

He reached over and opened the door just behind him—and I thought *he* smelled bad. In came the aroma of a barnyard with its cud-chewing cows with swarming flys, high-strung pecking chickens and moldy piles of blackening hay that imparted a biting sting to my nostrils. "I guess you could say 'farm hand'."

"You spent many years at Sunstone Laboratories, a

company highly respected in the community, so what happened?"

"Screw 'em. Screw 'em all! They don't deserve *my*
respect."

"You didn't do something to bring down the research
center did you?"

"Me, hell no. We had great project on plate. Revolution-
ize everyday lives. We solve the tissue problem, build successful carbon regenerating plant. We were to introduce to
world a fantastic prototype. But no! Montford Fouquet, he
had converse idea about ultimate utility.

"Fouquet had a different use for your invention?"

"I think that's what I said."

"Yes sir, you did. What about Stuart and Wagner?"

"I no problem with them. Norman most levelheaded scientist on team, kept research on practical applications. Wilhelm, he keep us converged so we don't stray off primary
goal."

"But Fouquet—"

Fouquet, the sons-a-bitch, if not for him, this job like mine
no longer need. Ironic no?"

"I don't understand?"

"It would solve a lot of world's problems, but we had to be
careful, there was potential bad side."

"And that was?"

"Screw 'em, if not for Fouquet scheming to get us all
removed…he took on himself to destroy my reputation.
Look at me now."—Stravinsky poured some beer into the
palm of his hand and washed his face with it, and then continued—"I leave my family behind in East Berlin. I had to
leave; I no could do what Politburo wanted of me. No, I not
destroy world with biological weapons, not me. Be nothing
but rotting carcasses in city after city of whole world. I no
do it."

I was beginning to feel ill, what was happening? Was I

into something *way* over my head? Stravinsky was rambling on—he had loosened up—but I wasn't getting to the answers I was looking for.

"Boris…" I dared to use his first name.

"I lose my wife, two daughters…"

"Doctor! What happened to Sunstone Laboratories?"

"Sunstone blow up! To nothing. All our work! All our records, prototypes, computer files, equations. Some of us, we try reconstruct our records on our own. I keep in touch with Wagner and Stuart for long time. I think Wagner is only one still trying to solve his part of problem. He has the…"

"Equation?"

Blam! Suddenly, something exploded! Blood splat onto my eyeballs, chunks of meat slammed into my face, and everything went dark for a moment.

As my vision cleared, I saw that Stravinsky had no face! Red mushy flesh dangled from where his nose and cheeks had been just moments before. An eyeball hung from an eye-socket. His beer crashed to the floor. The Doctor fell forward onto the table revealing a neat round hole in the back of his head. It squirted bright red blood and a river of hemoglobin quickly overran the table. The yellow walls, the dishes, and my clothes were splattered with blood and pieces of—aaaah! I threw up into the puddle of blood and then threw up again.

My attention was brought to the sound of footsteps creaking on the wood floor above me. I shook my head trying to get my wits about me and wiped my face with my handkerchief. A moving shadow got my attention: a man had crossed in front of the window. Suddenly, the window shattered and I heard a bullet whiz by me. That was good, that I *heard* it; if you hear it, it *didn't* hit you. I knew that from boot camp—on the firing range—where you had to, with a fellow trainee, work your way down the course giving each other cover while you shot at pop-up targets in the shape of men.

You were using real ammunition, a .45 long in an M16-A1, an automatic weapon that could be set for single fire—thirty cartridges to a magazine—but the ammunition didn't last long if you used it improperly. The drill sergeant taught us to press on the trigger and quickly release it, allowing a burst of three shots; hold it any longer and your weapon was dangerously hot and your magazine deadly empty. The sound of a bullet passing by you was sobering. My first experience with flying bullets was in a trench at the back of the firing range: I was crouched down in front of the berm that caught the bullets and cringed as bullets whizzed just over my head—very sobering indeed.

Another shot rang out.

I slid to the floor. This was no boot camp, no trench to duck into…no…someone meant to kill me.

I made my way over to the kitchen window, leaned over the bloody sink, and carefully looked out. I was considering the window as a possible way out. I grabbed the brass lever and pushed the window open slowly. There was a dull-orange barrel-tile roof just below the window.

The knob slowly turned on the door to the barnyard.

I wasted no time climbing out of the window.

twelve

THE TILES were slippery. I had to climb onto a higher roof and climbed toward the ridge to get my bearings. Roof lines shot off in every direction—additions added to additions—and there were no right angles; buildings were laid every which way, their irregularity made them an artist's dream, but hard as hell to navigate. Clotheslines hung outside second-story windows and flower boxes with yellow and white tulips hung in front of others. I heard a roof tile slide.

I scrunched low and peeked over the ridge.

It was Branko Tanovic—the huge Slav—he was climbing toward me.

I froze.

thirteen

NOT A MUSCLE moved in my body as Tanovic reached the ridge of the roof, standing there, towering over me. He had a gun in his hand, a Russian 9mm Makarov. My heart pounded. Could he hear it? I tried to stop it from hammering, but it only pounded that much faster. About right now, I thought, I would prefer bullets whistling *past* my head. The tiles creaked above me. I took a deep breath—possibly my last—and reached up to grab his leg and yanked on it, hard. Tanovic fell backward and dropped his pistol. He slid head long down the opposite slope of the gable roof. The gun followed him. Tanovic slid off the roof, head first, into the barnyard beyond. His gun dropped into the gutter.

The gun!

I shinnied over the ridge and quickly down to the gutter. Kneeling, I reached for the gun, searching frantically through putrefied leaves. A hairy hand grabbed the gutter, and then another hand, and the gutter creaked as the Yugoslavian's yellowish-brown face popped into view. I stared at him. He stared back. And then he began to grin an awful, crooked, crap-eating smirk. I continued to feel for the gun—and found it. I brought it up to Tanovic, pointing it at his ugly face.

Tanovic stared for a moment, then released his hands and dropped into a haystack below. He then ran across the chicken-infested barnyard, squawking hens scurrying around wildly.

I followed him; *I* had the Makarov now. Maybe this cabbagehead could tell me what was going on. I wasn't afraid to confront him; I knew his weakness.

Buildings surrounded the barnyard, with only a small gateway to the street. The cows brayed as Tanovic reached the gate, but the doors were barred shut. He fumbled with the lock, but as I approached, he turned and ran through a shed of hanging tobacco leaves and turned back to upset a wooden cart loaded with wine barrels. As I jumped over a barrel that was rolling toward me, he grabbed a ladder hanging horizontally on a wall and swung it at me. I ducked and threw a bucket of freshly-picked day lilies at him. The lilies, and a half-gallon of water, washed over his ugly face. I pushed him into a stack of burlap bags full of potatoes— hard potatoes. He grabbed a pitchfork. I backed off.

He then ran across the yard to the entrance of the living quarters and found the door unlocked. I followed, close on his heels. We found ourselves in the farmhouse living room. *"Was der Hölle!"* screamed a woman as she dropped a load of dirty dishes. Her husband just sat there watching television in his sleeveless undershirt—a shirt that didn't quite cover his hairy beer belly.

Tanovic tore his way through the front door and ran onto the street. He scurried like a scared rabbit, but I stayed close behind; I had the size and age advantage. Tanovic slipped on the uneven cobblestones; I could tell he was exhausted. He slammed into a deliveryman carrying a stack of red-plastic beer cases. He, and the cases, went flying, broken bottles and foaming beer flowing down the street, soon to make the neighborhood cats and dogs smile. Tanovic got to his feet and climbed over the deliveryman who then got to his feet, blocking my way.

The Slav disappeared around a corner.

I rounded the corner just as a car screeched to a halt, just missing Tanovic who ran cattycorner across the street. I raised the Makarov to shoot and a young woman stepped out of a doorway into the line of fire—I had already pulled the trigger. The woman dropped her basket of eggs. They splat on the pavement as she went weak-kneed, fell back against the door, and slid slowly to the ground.

I rushed up to her. She looked at me strangely. Her eyes said she didn't understand what had happened to her. I couldn't see into those eyes, they were dark and hollow. The shades were coming down. The color in her face was fading. And my stomach was knotting up—tighter—and tighter.

I looked down the street for Tanovic.

He was gone.

I made a decision to leave the dying woman and ran to the intersection. I couldn't let him get away, not now. I was in deep dung. Fear in the form of cold sweat was racing down my face. I wiped it with my sleeve and looked left and then right. There he was—for an instant—and then he disappeared down an alleyway. I ran after him.

I turned into the alley only to be confronted with a six-foot wood-slat fence. A trash can was rolling away from it. Tanovic was close—just on the other side of that hurdle; I was sure of it. I pulled a crate in front of the fence, stepped back for a running start, barreled forward, planted my left foot on the box, and leaped over the fence. But I came down hard on a pile of bricks and felt my shinbones crack.

The burly Yugoslavian, out of breath, stopped at the end of the alley and bent over and wiped his brow and then looked back at me—he then grinned and slipped around the corner.

I, with my aching legs, entered the street in time to see

Tanovic approaching a man riding toward us on a bicycle. Tanovic kicked at the bicycle sending the man cartwheeling to the pavement. The bicycle gyrated wildly and eventually slammed to the ground. Tanovic picked up the two-wheeler, turned it around and hopped on. I would have laughed at the big baboon on the small bike—front wheel wobbling as he tried to get up enough speed to balance the blasted thing— if it hadn't been for the fact that the son-of-a-bitch had just tried to kill me.

I was gaining on him, just a few steps behind him now, reaching out for the bicycle, but he was accelerating away from me and had time to look back at me and grin. That pissed me off.

I reached for my gun—Tanovic's Makarov.

I took aim.

Tanovic entered a street intersection. Tires squealed as a car braked—a chrome grill slammed into the brawny Yugoslavian. His bicycle came to a stop instantly and Tanovic continued onto the windshield, cracking it like a frozen lake in the spring time. Two men clamored out of a black Mercedes-Benz; one was the greasy-haired throat strangler from the train—I'll call him Roach, short for cockroach, a most apropos name for the blood-sucking leech. Other drivers screamed to a halt and began to exit their vehicles. Roach pulled Tanovic off the hood, springing the hood ornament over on its side; if not for the spring it would have been sheared off. The driver of the Benz, a tall, lanky guy, looking like an undernourished ferret, snapped the twinkling hood ornament back in place, more concerned about it than Tanovic.

I approached with gun in hand.

Tanovic had forgotten about me and was cussing a blue streak, but the ferret saw me and drew his automatic pistol. I dived for cover behind a trash can. Ough! Unless it's into water, diving is hard on the hands and knees.

Just then, a police car slid in between the henchmen and myself. Two uniformed men jumped out as bullets pierced the side of their Cop Beetle. A firestorm of bullets screamed through the air. All hell had broken loose. Pedestrians went scampering as hot lead pounded the surrounding buildings—shards of window glass took flight, crashing to the pavement below.

I cowered in a doorway.

Traffic was beginning to jam up like logs on a narrowing river. Pedestrians were getting in the line of fire and the police were forced to stop shooting. I slunk lower into the doorway. What had I gotten myself into? I curled up in the corner—the Makarov held to my face as I tried to shield myself from stray bullets. I felt helpless. I felt guilty. And I felt small.

fourteen

BULLETS CRACKED around me, but I didn't hear them. I had just wanted to play detective, thought it would be a kick. But now I was in the middle of a gun battle—and this wasn't in the jungles of Vietnam. But I *was* in a foreign country, far from home. I might never see Buffalo again, just a dark and dank jail cell. The bewildered woman's face—her lifeblood draining away—crawled back into my consciousness: I had killed an innocent woman! It was the cooler for me with rats for lunch, cockroaches for dessert and a rock for a pillow. And maybe, if I'm lucky, they'll give me a tin cup to piss in and a stinking pot to crap in. Hopefully they'd be nice enough to empty the pot at least once a day.

The pistol was pulled away from my face and a hand grabbed me under the arm and jerked me upward. I peered into the eyes of a familiar face. It was Inspector Gerhard Schultz. Boy, was I glad to see him, and how nice for him to come all the way from Heidelberg to see me. But around him stood numerous frowning men in their intimidating gray Gestapo uniforms.

I swallowed hard and asked, "Did you get 'em?"

Schultz just shook his head, and then said, "Got away."

"Got away! How?" I looked about; the crowd was closing in. People peered curiously out of their open windows. A man carried his son on his shoulders and an old woman calmly pushing a cart full of fresh produce passed us as if nothing unusual had taken place. Maybe it hadn't. Nothing made sense to me. A choking crowd of people and this was no spring harvest parade.

The cops handcuffed me and walked me out to the street.

"How in Christ did they get away?" I asked again as they pushed me into a Volkswagen with a siren and blue bubble on top.

We drove off.

An ambulance passed us.

fifteen

*B*ITTE *nehmen Sie Platz.*"

I sat down.

"You like it here, Mr. Noble?" asked the Inspector as he laid his orange sunglasses on the wooden table in front of me. "I see you're having fun at our expense.

What do you think you're doing? Everywhere you go I find bodies—dead ones. Dr. Stuart, Dr. Stravinsky, and now young woman—and by the way—her name was *Fraülein* Elfie Detrich. Should I know something, Mr. Noble? Why these men after you?"

"Beats me," I said as I peered at myself in the mirror on the opposite wall. Of course, I knew it wasn't just a mirror, it was a one-way mirror; the Gestapo was back there watching me. My goose was cooked.

"Why you not know?" asked the Inspector, his voice rising one octave.

"I was just trying to find the scientists who had worked with Professor Wagner."

"You found them."

"I haven't found Wagner."

"That's not your job. Get it out of your head."

"Have you received a ransom demand?"

"Is none of your business."

"Is Erika okay?"

"*She* is none of your business; stay away from her! *Verstehen*?"

"*Ich verstehe.*"

Inspector Schultz slammed down my brown envelope with 'ERIKA' lettered on it. "*Was ist das*?"

"My notes."

Schultz pulled the contents from the envelope, leaving the black & white 8 x 10 on top—with a big black "X" marked over the face of Doctor Stuart. "You did not mark over Stravinsky's face. Explain, please."

"Didn't have a chance."

The Inspector slammed his hand down on the table.

"You're a funny man, Mr. Noble…Explain!"

"I'm a reporter, got to keep rec…"

"*Bin ich blöd*? You think I stupid? I look into you. I call *die Bild-Zeitung*; they never hear of you. You no work for them.

You get your jolly off this kind of *scheisse*…"

"No, sir. I work freelance. I'm getting an edu…"

"Your ass-hole's sucking wind."

"Inspector, these men were working on some kind of top-secret project together. I think it could be very big."

"Big?" He pulled a chair out and sat down across from me. "I'm listening. If you lie, *Gefängnis*!"

"Jail! I'm being straight with you. There's hints of something big, like the way Stravinsky talked about the project."

"What are you talking about?"

"I don't know, but that's why I'm so curious."

"Curious! Friggin' curious killed the friggin' cat."

Schultz paused, letting his blood pressure lower a bit.

"*Dunlops*. Two-oh-five-seventy-R-fourteens," said Scultz.

"What?"

"The tire prints in Berlin—from the black Mercedes—they match the prints we found at the Wagner mansion. We fairly certain goons that killed Stravinsky also did Wagner kidnapping. We have their plates. The Benz is registered to a Jake Finger and the big ape you were chasing, probably a Yugoslavian transplant. We got lot of them because of labor shortage in Germany.

"He's Branko Tanovic."

"Who?"

"Branko Tanovic, I had a few words with him on the train."

"*Wartezeit*! Wait just a damn minute, Mr. Noble, start from beginning, tell me everything you know, everything that was said." The Inspector opened a hand-carved mahogany box and removed a Cuban cigar.

"Can I get you something, a soda perhaps?"

"Sure, a *Coca-Cola*. I'm awfully thirsty."

The Inspector bit off the the end, lit his cigar, and took a puff; a billow of smoke rose to the ceiling. "Not until you spill guts."

That did it! That sent me back to the sight of Stravinsky's brain as it blew into my face. Pieces of him everywhere. Blood exploding all over the puke-yellow room. "Inspector, you don't know what I've been through."

"You are crazy mixed-up kid—from United States no less. When was last time citizens die for freedom on your friggin' soil?"

I shot back: "When was the last time *your* people were trying to take the freedom away from the rest of us? Have you forgotten World War II, *Herr* Schultz?"

The inspector said nothing for a moment and then he spoke with uncontrolled furry, "We've no freedom as long as we can't walk the streets and feel safe. That's the bottom line isn't it? Freedom is feeling safe. *Fraülein* Detrich felt safe when she walked out her friggin' door with a basket of hen eggs. But she wasn't safe, now was she? WAS SHE?"

"No sir."

"Then, my friend, you're part of the problem—no?"—I slumped in my chair—"Besides, do I have blond hair and blue eyes?…You screw up, my friend. Step on dick, as you American's say. Stand up, Noble, turn around." He picked up a key and removed the cuffs from my wrists. "I notice eggshells stuck in soles of your shoes. You should walk lightly my friend." He looked me straight in the eyes. "You should be straight with me—and most important, you should be straight with yourself. If you don't, you end up in *Leichenwagen.*"

"In what?"

"How you call it…a hearse? You're, how you say, responsibility in this incident is not clear, but I'm not going to hold you. I'm letting you go Mr. Noble, I owe you one. You've called in your marker so don't expect any more favors—now get to hell out of here! Get your sorry ass back to Heidelberg and leave me to Wagner."

I slid my chair aside and headed for the door, my head hanging low, very low.

"Mr. Noble!"

"Sir?"

"I not tell you, *Fraülein* Detrich's not dead. Yes, she's still alive. Just a painful, gut wrenching, stomach wound. How's *your* stomach, Mr. Noble?"

sixteen

DAY FOUR. Friday, April 4th. I was back in Heidelberg; my mind was spinning. I had just survived another near death experience. I had survived Branko Tanovic, I had survived the German *Polizei*, and I had survived Gerhard Schultz. It was my *glücklich tag*, my lucky day. But Schultz had let me go much too easily. Sure the gun I used wasn't mine, sure it was Tanovic who murdered Stravinsky, and sure Tanovic shot at me first, but Schultz could have jailed me for any number of violations of German law, so why did he let me go? I looked in my rearview mirror. Maybe Schultz was following me, letting me go so I could serve as bait to catch the thugs. I looked back again: no one was there. Maybe he didn't think I would make a good night crawler.

And now I was asking for more trouble: I was driving back to Schwetzingen, back to see Erika. I thought I should tell her what happened, tell her I was okay and tell her I hadn't found her father. Maybe I just wanted someone to talk to, maybe I just wanted to see her.

I drove through the iron gate and up to the front door. Erika opened the door as if expecting me. She reached forward and hugged me around the neck.

"I heard what happened…in Berlin. Are you all right?"

"I'm fine, no big deal," I said, feigning bravery.

"I should have gone with you."

"I'm very glad you didn't."

Erika pulled me into the drawing room. "Care for some tea?"

"That would be nice."

"Let me put the water on."

Erika returned shortly and abruptly said, "You must find my father. The police are not making any progress."

"They are, it just takes time."

"Time. My father may not have time."

"They now have the names of two of the kidnappers," I added.

"They do?"

"Yes, but none of it makes sense. Why did they kidnap your father? There's still no ransom demand. Nothing quite fits together, like pieces from two different jigsaw puzzles."

"Maybe they want what he knows," said Erika.

"Trying to get something from him, like a certain equation?"

"Yes, an equation; he *is,* you know, a scientist."

"Yes, but what field? That I don't know."

"He's a physicist and a biochemist."

"Working in his home in a crude laboratory? I don't think so. It's just a cover for something else. He's working on something important, and whatever it is, it's big."

"I don't understand?"

"Large in scope, earth shaking, maybe involves a lot of people—dangerous people. I already know some of them. People are killing each other over this 'big' thing, and, they're shooting at me, little old me! That's what I mean by something big."

"Oh."

"Yeah, and I've got the Inspector on my tail too."

Erika tilted her head like a perplexed dog.

"The inspector *insisted* I stay out of this mess," I continued.

"My father's in danger, and you're the one that's done the most to find him."

"That's not true…and I've no more leads to follow."

"Brandon, please!" Erika sat down beside me.

"You've got to understand, I nearly killed a woman."

"The woman on the news? In Berlin?"

"Yes, Elfie Detrich was…is her name."

"No, not you. You're too sweet." Erika leaned forward and smacked a honey-sweet kiss on my blushing cheek.

seventeen

ERIKA and I cruised along the French countryside in my Volkswagen. We were off the lightning-fast autobahn and were enjoying the countryside, cruising on a two-lane road flanked with gorgeous old trees bowing gracefully over the road. Erika had her window down, the slipstream caressing her beautiful hair. I was glad she had come along, though it was actually she who had insisted. I figured Montford Fouquet was my only hope for some clue to Wagner's whereabouts. Stravinsky, before he took a bullet—maybe meant for me—had pointed his finger back at Fouquet for breaking up the research team.

It would've been nice if we were in a sleek 280SL Mercedes with the top down, instead of my old egg-shaped VW. A beautiful girl in a beautiful car in a wonderfully romantic French countryside, I had everything but the great car.

Suddenly, the generator discharge light flickered and

then rose to a steady red glow. I pulled to the side of the road and coasted to a stop. I climbed from the car and opened the engine lid. There was the problem.

"We'll be here a few minutes Erika, hop on out, get a breath of fresh air."

"Is it petrol?"

"No, I've got to change the brushes in the generator."

"Brushes, for the hair?" she asked.

"No, generator brushes. This old generator wears them down fast."

"You can fix that here?"

"Sure, it's a VW. I can actually replace the brushes without pulling out the generator. I could change the oil right here; I could change the fan belt, even change the…"

"Then you can fix me."

"Fix you?"

"You can tie up my hair for me."

"Okay, sure," I said. Here I was trying to get us on the road again and she wanted her hair up. Women, go figure.

"You're a handy man to have around," Erika said cutely.

My ego soared.

Under the bonnet, I had all the spare parts I might need for roadside repair. The extra brushes would once again come in handy.

"I like your hair," cooed Erika softly as she ran her fingers through my hair while I knelt down in front of the engine and slipped the spring off one of the brushes.

Erika ran her hands along my shoulders. "You've got such a muscular body."

What was she up to, I wondered, as I took my needle-nose pliers and lifted a brush out, taking care not to drop the brush into the generator.

"You're being awfully flirtatious, Miss Wagner," I said. "Why don't you take a walk down the road, I'll pick you up in a few minutes."

"That's okay, I like watching you work."

That was enough, she was up to something. No woman likes to watch a man work. I replaced the second brush. In less than fifteen minutes we were off and running again. Erika got her hair tied up, though maybe I got a little grease on it.

I pulled into the driveway of Fouquet's imposing château and hurried around to open the door for Erika. She angled her bare knees out of the tiny cockpit. The beetle was big by European standards, but it wasn't made for long-legged women, especially pretty, proper ones. I couldn't help but watch her every graceful move. Her high heels were spotless and looked expensive. Her silk stockings shined as if a bright, focused light was shining on them. Today she wore a more casual outfit than usual—a red skirt and a blazer over a white cashmere sweater—but in no way was she casual. Her makeup looked perfect—if she wore any at all—her eyelashes long, but not too long. All natural I figured, all of her.

We climbed a long row of steps to the front door and rang the bell. A gargoyle, looking like a monstrous dragon, stared down at us from the archway.

"I hope I can be of service to you, Mr. Noble," said Erika.

"I'm hoping you can observe his reactions to my questions and tell me if he's being truthful."

"I'll try."

"And he'll be distracted by your beauty and might let his guard down."

I rang the doorbell again.

"Maybe seeing him will jar some memories."

"If I have any; I don't remember much about him."

I pushed the button once again. There seemed to be no activity. I grabbed the doorknob and turned it. The door came open.

We entered into the huge foyer. The knight's armor was gone; only the oak platform remained.

Erika's heels echoed about the large hall. We entered the first room and found all the furniture draped with white furniture covers. Several oil paintings that looked like originals, hung from picture moldings high on the walls.

We headed for the game room, the one place I remembered. The billiard table was gone, the carpet darker in color where the table had been. And the framed photos and diplomas, they were also missing.

"Mr. Noble, come here." I turned to find Erika kneeling on the floor. It looked so unlike her.

"Can you see the footsteps, Brandon. They go straight toward that paneled wall."

"I can see them." I approached the wall and looked around. There was no door, but I felt cool air seeping from around the moulding. I felt around the edges looking for a release lever—nothing—I started pulling on books in an adjacent bookshelf. "I saw that in a movie," I said. "A book was the secret lever."

But none of the books activated anything. Erika reached up to a painting hanging on the wall and pulled down on one edge of it, it tilted, there was a deep raking sound behind the wall and a section of the wall opened up. I marveled at it. A house with secret passages, I had never seen one. As a kid, I wanted to live in a house with secret passageways to all the rooms. And now, here was a hidden door that led to a stairway leading downward. It was time to explore, so down we went. We soon came upon a wine cellar. I had hoped for something more, a dungeon maybe, a counterfeit printing operation perhaps, but no, nothing of the sort, just bottles of wine nestled in cherrywood racks. I pulled one out. *"Möet & Chandon, Epernay, France,* good champagne I'm told, the best."

I pulled two wooden crates out into the middle of the room and found a case of crystalline champagne glasses and handed one to Erika. "Care for a drink?" I twisted on the plastic cork; it suddenly blew to the ceiling. The bottle bubbled with foam and spit sparkling fizz.

Erika laughed. Yeah, she actually laughed; the first time I'd seen her really cheerful.

Plunk, plunk, there was a noise on the floor above, and the sound of footsteps.

Shrumps, a bar lock slid shut.

I dashed up the cellar stairs—the champagne bottle still in hand—and pushed on the door. It didn't budge. I pushed again, harder. I stopped to listen for noises outside and then turned to look at Erika down below. Her big eyes stared up at me puzzled, her empty glass still held up in her hand. I realized I hadn't poured the champagne yet and returned to the cellar. I took Erika's glass and carefully poured a small amount. Erika smiled.

"Well, try it," I said.

"Um, okay."

"You like champagne don't you?"

"Well, not really."

"Does it give you a headache, a lot of people get headaches from champagne."

"They do?"

Erika took a tiny sip of the champagne. She smiled mysteriously.

"Um, I do think I'm getting a headache."

"Already?"

"Uh-huh." She looked seductively into my eyes. I was mesmerized. Her beautiful chestnut eyes stayed fixed on mine. I looked at her long eyelashes. I looked at her thin, perfectly shaped eyebrows and the supple, flawless skin. She was standing very close to me. I was within her zone of intimacy and could smell her lovely body perfume. Then, out of the blue, I said something stupid: "I don't want you to get a headache."

Erika took another sip. "Um, it's good," she said in a delicate, sweet voice.

Chair legs screeched across the floor above and a television set was clicked on. An afternoon soap opera boomed.

eighteen

A TELEPHONE rang upstairs, then two rings, three rings; the handset was lifted, *Jawohl!* I could hear a muffled German conversation and then the handset was returned to the telephone and the chair slid again on the wood floor.

I decided it was time to find a defensive position and looked for a place to hide. I grabbed the confused Erika and pulled her behind the wine rack. I took a wine bottle by its neck, a weapon if need be. The door's bolt slid open, the door opened, light streamed down the stairs. A short, greasy-haired man stepped carefully down the stairs. It was Roach, the henchman in Berlin, the same cockroach who tried to knife me on the train. My heart was in my throat; I ducked lower. Roach scanned the room, listening; he didn't see us. He pulled his Arkansas Toothpick from a sheath on his leg and moved about the room, looking and listening. He walked to one of the wine racks and pushed on a latch. The rack swung outward, and behind it was a tunnel. Roach looked around the room once more, then headed into the opening.

"Come on," I whispered to Erika. We followed Roach into the passageway and made our way down a small, dimly lit tunnel that was chiseled through solid rock. Bare light bulbs were strung along the ceiling of the passageway. Dripping water echoed a hollow eerie sound. We approached narrow steps that lead farther downward, and following them, we came to a metal door. We opened it and a rush of cold air and glaring light welcomed us. In the brightly-lit room, fluorescent lights hummed overhead. It was a large, rectangular room sheathed in tin. I felt like I was inside a huge rotisserie oven.

The room smelled of ether, maybe chloroform, and the biting smell of alcohol. Or maybe it was the smell of death: formaldehyde. Electrical outlet boxes on black power cords dangled over several stainless-steel, slab-like tables aligned like dominos across the room. White sheets covered what looked like human forms. The room resembled a morgue. I approached one of the tables and slowly lifted one of the sheets. There, a man lying face down, buck-naked, his skin wrinkled and pale. I lifted another sheet: another body lying face up, a young man with dark hair. His glassy lifeless eyes were wide open, staring up at the ceiling. My skin began to crawl. I touched his arm. It was neither cold nor warm, just room temperature.

Erika and I moved through another doorway. Erika screamed as a hairy, beastly hand fell on her shoulder. I pulled her to me. There, behind her, shackled along the wall were several grotesque creatures. One was a hairy, deformed body of swollen flesh. A human once upon a time maybe. It appeared to be unconscious, maybe even dead. And next to this monster was another distorted body, that of a nude female with very long straw-blond hair—but matted, frayed, and disheveled—and her face was badly bruised... she jerked.

"Oh my heavens!" cried Erika, bringing her hands to her mouth, her eyes wide with astonishment. "She's alive!"

I approached the female and tried to raise her drooping head. Her eyes were closed. I held her face and tried to open an eyelid. Her eyeball was fixed and dilated.

Suddenly Erika screamed out. I left my shorts behind and may have left something in them. I turned to see Roach with his knife poised at Erika's neck. Roach pulled her close to him, his face against hers. She trembled.

"Don't make a move, Noble, unless you want to see her beautiful neck ripped wide open, her juggler floppin' 'round like a spaghetti noodle."

I raised my hands to gesture my submission; I didn't want him to do anything rash, I had seen enough blood. I sure didn't want to see Erika's. Roach walked Erika further into the room. I noticed that there were other shackles attached to the walls. Here was the dungeon I had hoped for, but now I wasn't so glad I'd found it.

"Get over against that wall, Noble."

I circled to the wall; Roach kept his eyes fixed on me.

"Against the wall, put your hands in those irons...do it!"

I obliged without hesitation.

"Snap them shut!"

At that, I hesitated. I saw a horrific, deformed creature moving behind Roach—approaching him slowly—right out of an old 1950's horror movie.

"What is this all about?" I asked.

"Shut up and lock those irons!"

The monster grabbed Roach around the neck. Roach, surprised, lost his grip on Erika, and she dashed to me as Roach turned to the hairy creature and jabbed his knife into it. The monster's other ugly, misshapen arm circled Roach's body and squeezed. Roach's face turned lobster red. The monster squeezed tighter. Any moment now, I was sure his head would pop like a juicy zit. Roach found himself in a powerful vice and he knew he was in a tight situation. Suddenly, his head was forced backward, careening his neck almost to its breaking point. He gasped for air. He tried to stab the monster again, the long knife sliding into the creature's gut. Then I heard Roach's neck snap; his hands went limp, his arms fell lifelessly to his side, and his eyes fell back in his head exposing the white of his eyeballs. He was dead.

Erika stood in shock, motionless, nailed to the floor. The creature stared at us. I grabbed Erika's hand and pulled her back into the first room. We climbed the steps in the tunnel passageway, returned to the wine cellar, climbed the stairs, passed through the game room, crossed the hall, ran through the foyer, and tore through the front door as fast as our legs could carry us.

The black Mercedes—the same blasted Benz with cracked windshield—slid to a halt in front of us. The doors were flung open.

I released Erika yelling "run, get in my car."

The stout Yugoslavian, Branko Tanovic, approached me with that mean-spirited grin on his face. I didn't waste any time; I went straight for his nuts, my insole hard to the groin. He buckled over in pain. I grinned. What a big wimp, I thought. Then the other man came up behind me; it was the ferret, Jake Finger. I bent my knees, grabbed him low, and used his forward momentum to pull him over the top of me, landing him on the hood of the Mercedes and in the process snapping the hood ornament off the car. He rolled off the hood and fell on top of Tanovic. I ran for my VW, started the car, and shifted into gear. Just then, Tanovic's hand grabbed my door handle. The door came open as my VW lurched forward, but the burly Slav lost his grip and fell to the ground.

I drove out the iron gate.

nineteen

I LOOKED in my rear-view mirror to see the black Mercedes looming large, barreling toward me. Erika looked at me as if she was just along for the ride—a ride I knew wasn't going be much fun. I had to lose the Mercedes, the sooner the better.

But the Benz was determined to catch us, sooner or later.

I shifted into third and made a hard right turn down a narrow one-way street. Cars were parked halfway on the sidewalk on my left. I kept my eyes open for pedestrians as I zipped down the street. The ominous black Benz was still hot on my tail. Up ahead, a car moved into my lane at a cross street. I jerked my steering wheel to miss it. After I passed, the car then continued into the street blocking the Benz. The Benz hit its brakes hard, skidding on the cobblestone pavement and hitting the side of the intruding car near its front end, causing it to spin around. The Benz driver then floored it again, but passed the street I had just turned on, and realizing his mistake, made a skidding U-turn, hitting a parked car.

I raced out of town through a stone archway and I dropped my stick into forth. I found myself on a narrow dirt road passing a dung wagon, passing a tractor hobbling along at three-k's-per-hour, and passing a meandering bicyclist who thought he owned the whole damn road.

"What do these men want with us?" asked Erika abruptly.

"I think they mean to kill us."

"But why?" asked Erika.

"The devil's in the details."

The black Benz was again in my rear-view mirror.

I found myself on a winding mountain road sprinkled with hairpin turns. A bullet hit my rear window and broke it into thousands of glistening cubes of glass. My VW kissed the cliff's edge as I attempted to negotiate the turns even faster.

Another bullet took out my radio antenna. I looked to my rear to see Jake Finger in the driver's seat as Tanovic stared at me—grinning. I entered a curve and slid through it and the Benz followed, but it too slid successfully through it. I had hoped they wouldn't make it.

A couple more tight turns and I appeared to be gaining ground. As the Benz fell further behind, it disappeared from view.

"I think we've got it made," I said hopefully as I looked over to Erika…but she wasn't there.

"I'm here," said Erika as she pulled herself up from the footwell and brushed back her hair.

"You okay?" I asked.

"Yes, but maybe I should stay down here."

"Maybe you shou…" I hit the brakes hard.

Appearing unexpectedly, the black Mercedes darted out of a side road just in front of us. To avoid him, I veered off the road into the woods, but the Benz followed us. My VW bounced wildly on the rough ground and my head hit the roof with several good twangs. Tree limbs scraped the sides of my bug and tree trunks rushed at us like an army intent on destruction. Then we saw daylight as we entered a clearing. A young couple bolted from a blanket where they were making out, and an ice chest flew into the air splattering soft drinks on my windshield.

The Mercedes came around trying to cut us off. The scene looked like two serpents—one white one black—slithering through the grass playing cat and mouse. The young couple scurried toward their car and just as they were about to reach it, the Benz broadsided it, pushing it into a tree. The Benz had to back up. That gave me time to find a road that led away from the clearing. Soon, we were back on the mountain road, a steep cliff dropping off to our right.

"I think we're clear of them," I said.

"Well, ease up then. My knuckles don't match the rest of my skin—they're white."

I raised my foot slightly off the gas pedal. "There, is that better?" I asked.

"I don't think I'm going to ride with you ever again," replied Erika.

Suddenly, the Mercedes rammed into my rear. My head lurched violently backward. Erika grabbed the steering wheel to keep us away from the cliff's edge.

I regained control.

The Benz came alongside me, scraping my fenders. It tried to push me to the right—over the edge. Sounds of crunching, grinding metal and my left rear fender was ripped off and the front fender ground against the tire causing it to smoke with a burning-rubber stinch. Erika glared disapprovingly at the men in the offending car.

"Erika, open the glove box, hand me that wrench."

She handed me a large crescent wrench.

I took a firm grip and threw the wrench at Tanovic. It hit him squarely in the face. He bounced and struck the driver obliquely. The Benz veered right, hitting me first, and then it careened left and hit the stone wall. Tanovic grabbed his bloodied head. I could see Finger fighting to regain control of his vehicle. The Benz veered into me again, the battered passenger door came open, and Tanovic fell out, his body tumbling back between the vehicles like a floppy rag doll.

A panel truck was approaching from up ahead. There wasn't enough room on the road for the three of us. I hit my brakes and skidded and fought the wheel to stay on the road. The truck veered into the stone wall. The Benz braked, the harsh, hopeless sound of skidding wheels—then an awful silence—and then the metallic bang of crunching steel as the truck hit the Benz, hard. The truck careened off the Benz and went airborne—right over the cliff.

A big explosion from down below shook my car as I skidded into the Mercedes. The bonnet crumpled upward. A mushroom cloud of thick dust rose up over the cliff's edge and a clatter of metal rained to the earth. Then the world seemed eerily quiet. I heard my heart pounding, demanding to get out, but I was alive. I took a deep breath as the choking, dust-filled air began to clear. I looked out the side window and could see Jake Finger slumped over his steering wheel, his bloody hands still clutching the wheel. The windshield was shattered and Finger's head was mincemeat; it could have been canned without further processing.

I pulled Erika from the car on the driver's side because *her* door was hanging precariously over the cliff's edge. She was conscious and okay. I propped Erika against the side of the car and reached back in the car for my *Nikon*. I was hoping it wasn't broken after having been thrown violently around in the car. It looked okay, only a small dent on the edge of the filter on my wide-angle lens.

"What happened?" Erika asked, still confused.

"A little mishap." I stepped back and snapped two shots of the wreck and a third shot over the cliff's edge of the burning truck. I thought, I could really become a photojournalist. Then it hit me. Someone had been driving that truck and that someone would never ever drive anything again.

twenty

I APPROACHED Jake Finger, took his pulse, he was definitely dead, no purpose in pulling him from the wreck. I walked with Erika back down the road toward town. She was noticeably shaken and I wiped blood from her forehead. It was only a scratch, looked much worse than it was.

"Those bad men, do you think they're the ones that took my father?" Erika suddenly asked.

"I don't know."

"Why are those men after us?"

"I've no idea," I said, and I didn't. I was confused and tired. The 'bad men' seemed to be concerned about me and not Erika. They wanted to stop me, that was obvious, but from doing what? Did they think I knew too much? Knew something I actually didn't."

"Mr. Noble, look!" Erika stopped and pointed to bright blood droplets in the gravel. I kneeled down to take a closer look; it was fresh blood and it wasn't mine. I looked up. A searing pain came across my shoulder. The world went black as a cavern without lights.

twenty one

I WAS LOOKING through a blurry softness—like looking through the loose mesh of cheesecloth—and saw the face of a beautiful, dark, shadowy woman with high cheek bones, a small pert mouth, jet black hair, and penetrating eyes. The mirage then burned away into harsh white sunlight that glared into my eyes. I closed them to stop the pain. It was dark as a moonless night again.

twenty two

MY HEAD was swimming, my body floating. I couldn't clear my head. The room was shifting places, moving back and forth like the shimmering surface of a body of water and the image was broken into pieces like a jigsaw puzzle, each piece floating slowly in different directions. It was an understatement to say I was dizzy. I could hear an echo of voices in the room. My head ached. My shoulder blade hurt wretchedly. I heard the cracking sound of hard objects slamming into one another. I slowly opened my eyes, and in front of me was Montford Fouquet standing at his red billiard table. I looked around: his diplomas and medieval weapons weren't on the walls. I wasn't in his chateau. Fouquet bent over and fired the cue stick: the white cue ball hit the thirteen ball and went into a back pocket. He straightened back up and approached me, looking me over like I was the engine of a clunker on a used-car lot. I tried to raise my hands and found my wrists secured to wooden armrests with metal bracelets. I was in a large, straight-backed armchair made of heavy timbers and I was looking at Fouquet through a grid of iron bars. My head was in some kind of cage, like a birdcage, an iron framework hanging by a chain and secured around my chin with a steel neckstrap. A metal plate extended into my mouth and pressed down on my tongue. I couldn't speak; I couldn't even gurgle.

"It's a brank, Mr. Noble, for people who don't know how to mind their own business." He then turned to his manservant: "André, take it off so he can speak."

The well-dressed, expressionless André removed the padlock on the collar around my neck and lifted the contraption from my head.

"What is this all about?" I asked.

"You're getting my goat, Mr. Noble."

"Release me from this chair!"

"It's a ducking stool, Mr. Noble, used in the Middle Ages as a form of punishment. Hanging from a pole on a fulcrum, it could be lowered repeatedly into a river—a river of very cold water. Many malfactors died from the torture."

"What have I done?…Where am I?…What's going on around here?"

"Nothing that concerns you, Mr. Noble. You're screwing with Newton's First Law."

"What's that?" I asked as I squirmed in my chair.

"We were moving along just fine until you showed up."

"I don't know what you're talking about."

"That's good. And you should keep it that way. Go back to United States, Mr. Noble."

"I'm just trying to find Professor Wagner."

"He's none of your business. Leave him to the police."

"That's what *they* told me."

"Take their advice, Mr. Noble. Go home. Forces always act in pairs. You screw with me and I'll screw you right back…Newton's Third Law." Dr. Fouquet returned to his billiard table to complete his perfect run.

"How about Newton's *Second* Law, you skipped that one?"

"Thank you, Mr. Noble, it too will make good analogy in your case," replied Fouquet as he pulled a red billiard ball from under the table. "You're just one little infinitesimally insignificant little ball, Mr. Noble. If you hit me, I won't move very far, but if I hit you, you'd be history, Mr. Noble, just a flyspeck on wall, Newton's Second Law. UNDERSTAND?" He tossed the red ball and hit me in the sternum; the ball bounced off and rolled along the floor as I tried to catch my breath.

"I think I get the drift," I said.

"Good," said Montford Fouquet as he picked up his cue stick and took aim at the green-striped fourteen—it slammed neatly into a side pocket, but the cue ball came to rest behind the black eight ball blocking his shot on the fifteen, the last remaining ball. "Blast!"

He turned to André: "Take Mr. Noble away."

An outer door swung open and two men wearing white jackets entered. They removed the wrist shackles, took me by the arms, and lead me out of the room and down a long, very long, nondescript hallway. We turned down one corridor that angled off to the right and then down another hall to the left. I felt like a mouse in a maze. My legs felt rubbery; I was actually glad the two men were holding onto me. Two more men in civilian attire approached us and passed by. They looked like twins. I twisted to look back at them. They walked in step—left right, left right. I figured I was experiencing double vision. I felt drunk, weak-kneed, and drowsy. They must have drugged me.

The two men took me into a room—an operating room—with surgical tables and electronic gadgets hanging from the ceiling and the walls. They sat me up on one of the tables and I watched as a technician in a white lab coat walked over to what looked like a control panel with knobs and switches and VU meters. I took in the room: there was a long mirrored dressing table and what appeared to be barber chairs with headrests. On the table were groomed hairpieces on Styrofoam head molds, and makeup bottles and brushes, and head molds with latex masks of faces, but no eyes, just cut-outs for eyeballs.

The technician pulled on a large knife switch and locked it into its contacts. The panel hummed and lights flashed.

I looked around and saw a large window high on the wall and through reflections on the glass, was the woman I saw in my dream with her jet-black hair, high cheekbones, and a stern, sour look on her face—but oh, was she a knockout! She reminded me of my high school typing teacher: beautiful but all business, never the slightest grin on her sweet little mouth, a virgin who was still waiting.

I turned my head to another lab animal approaching me with a huge syringe, his fingers in the round holes of the retracted plunger. Light glinted off the needle as a drop appeared on its tip. I was feeling sick to my stomach. I tried to muster strength from deep within me. I thought of Erika. My eyes followed the needle as it approached the crook of my arm. I kicked outward and jumped to the floor. My left arm knocked the syringe out of the technician's hand and it clanged to the floor. I pushed the tech backward into the dressing table; hairpieces flew everywhere. I buckled to the floor bringing him with me. The syringe—lying quietly on the floor—stared me in the face. I reached for it and turned toward the tech. I brought the needle swiftly into his neck. His expression froze in utter surprise and bright blood spurted with a pulse like a lawn sprinkler. I twisted the needle and it snapped off in his neck and I let the syringe drop out of my hand, clanging again to the floor.

Blood covered my face and dripped into my eyes, blinding me as I pushed the gurgling tech off me.

I thought of Erika.

As I got to my feet, the second tech battered into me, pushing me against the operating table, and up over the top I went with a high flailing somersault—a bright light streaked past, then the casters of the table came into view. The tech came around the table and pounced down on me. My wind left me. I tried to breathe and couldn't, a heavy weight lay on my chest; my lungs would not take in air. But after what seemed like eternity, I sucked in a deep refreshing breath of air and tried to pull myself under the table—to safety—HELP, I wanted to scream out. A clinched fist hammered at my kidneys. I saw the feet of a third lab tech on the other side of the table. He began to bend over, to reach for me, but I grabbed his ankles and pulled. He fell backward into the control panel—it popped and sparkled—the room lights flickered and everything went dark except for the dancing flashes from the electrical shorts. The tech on top of me started to get up. I pushed the table at him; it hit him in the face. I clamored to my feet and grabbed the first thing I could feel, a heavy steel clamp—a chest retractor? an odd looking thing—and brought it across his already distressed face. His face was distorted badly by the weapon. I searched for the door, grabbed a handle and the hall light streamed into the room and across the bloody face of the second tech. I could see that his nose was gone.

I walked quickly down the hall straightening my clothes, unaware of the blood that might give me away. Around the corner approached two more technicians. I quickly turned into the nearest doorway and closed the door behind me. I found myself in a minimally lit lecture room, chairs anchored in a semi-circle around a large blackboard chalked with mathematical equations. A gray-haired man sat in a chair at the front, just in front of the podium. I slowly took the steps down to the front and approached the man. His head was down, unmoving. I came face to face with him and knelt down. He looked up at me. It was—

"Professor Wagner!"

He looked at me surprised.

"Are you okay, Doctor?"

"Who let you in here?" he asked.

"I'm, they're after…"

"How you get past guards?"

"Swiftly," I said.

"You're…you're Brandon Noble."

"Yes sir, photojournalist."

"You're American aren't you?"

"Uh, yes sir," *Why on God's green earth does everyone keep asking me that*, I thought, but said instead, "I came to get you out of here."

"It's too late, they have equation. They make me give it to them."

"What equation?" I asked. "The equation on the paper you burned up?"

"The solution, it's all they need."

"Solution, for what? And who is 'they'?" I asked, as I looked him squarely in the eyes.

"Doctor Fouquet, he want you out of way. I don't think he likes you."

"This is nuts!"

"He think you getting too close."

"Too close to what, for God's sake?"

"It is not so easy…where is my daughter?"

"She has been looking for you."

His eyes came sharply into focus, "Is she here?"

"Not here, but…"

"Is she all right?"

"She's fine," I said, not actually knowing what had happened to her. "Calm down, Doctor."

"You sure? My baby, you haven't done anything with her?"

"No sir, she's fine."

"You must find her. She's important to me."

"I'm sure, but how did…"

"Can you get me out of here?"

"Sir, I don't even know where we are, much less…"

"We're in research center."

"And where is that?"

"I show you. Come with me—put on that lab coat, look languid."

"Huh?"

"Don't show an expression."

"Why?"

"Do it!"

"What is this all abou…"

"Follow me."

We made our way down the hall, walking side by side, looking as if we belonged.

"Don't show any emotion on face, you'll fit in," he said. "They're bunch of Milquetoasts around here."

I looked at him strangely. Milquetoasts?

An approaching technician eyed me. I ignored him and stared straight ahead. The tech passed without incident.

"What is this place?" I asked.

"The new research center."

"Sunstone Laboratories?"

"Oh heavens no, my boy…here, come this way."

We entered another door, passed through a tunnel, went through a heavy steel door, and finally came to a huge boiler room. We climbed a long run of steel stairs and made our way along an overhead gangway, the boilers below us blowing hot steam. We ducked around asbestos-insulated piping and large valve handles like you might see in an old submarine to lock bulkhead doors. Hot steam was released across our path; we jumped and kept moving. It was the *Poseidon Adventure* all over again. I figured these boilers could heat this whole building even through the coldest of winters.

We approached a watchman asleep in an old oak desk chair with casters. We inched by him and over to a small window—the first window I had seen in a long time. It was dark outside, but the light from a full moon made the frosted windowpane glow brightly.

The watchman moved in his chair. I froze.

"You better take care of him," suggested the Doctor, casually indifferent.

I eyed him with dismay.

"Go on son, hit him over head."

I flinched—club a sleeping, man? This wasn't my idea of fair play.

"Go on!" the doctor nudged.

I quietly lifted the heavy black-iron *Underwood* typewriter on his roll-top desk and raised it above his head…but I hesitated. I couldn't hit him. Instead, I kicked at his chair and he jumped up hitting his own head on the typewriter, and back down he went, slumping peacefully over the desk.

The man was out cold.

"Come on, hurry up," nudged the doctor.

I placed the *Underwood* on the floor.

"In here, the bunkroom."

I followed him in.

"You can get sheets from the beds, tie them together."

"And?"

"You can't get out by gatehouse."

"Gatehouse?"

"Here," said the doctor as he unlatched, and pushed open the window.

I looked out…and down, way down. A large well-manicured grassy knoll lay before me. A tree line lay about seventy-five yards distant.

"You can get away through this window."

So we began to pull sheets from the bed, working quietly around a few sleeping men. I began to tie the sheets together, and soon, running short of sheets, I used white lab coats I found in the wall lockers. I looked through the window again and straight down and back again at the string of sheets. I held them up trying to estimate their length. "You think this is long enough?" I asked.

"I think so."

"You think so!"

"I can only estimate the drop, too many unknowns. Throw it down, it'll be fine, you'll see."

To many unknowns, I repeated to myself as I tied one end to a steam pipe and threw the bundle of sheets out the window. They unraveled downward and the end popped like a whip near the ground, but it didn't touch, it didn't hit the ground!

"I can't tell, I can't tell how far the end is off the ground!" I barked anxiously.

Clang-clang. Clang. Footsteps were pounding a path toward us along the expanded-metal gangway.

"We run out of time, go…you go first."

"Me!"

"Yes you. Now get out that window. You haven't a chance in here…"

I climbed onto the ledge and began to lower myself.

"I'll be safe, they still need me."

"What?"

"They need me for rest of equation—they won't hurt me. Go Mr. Noble, quickly!"

"Aren't you coming?"

He shook his head, "I can't make it down those bed sheets."

He wasn't coming with me. "Professor Wagner…"

"She's magnificent creature, no?"

"Who?"

"Erika, magnificent creature, you find her, take good care of her for me?"

"Yes," I said as I lowered myself slowly and carefully—the knots made good footholds. I looked back up at the Professor. He waved to me and smiled.

I reached the bottom of the rope of sheets and found that I was still at least ten feet from the ground, the ground still looking very distant. When I was up top, the sheet looked very close to the ground, but no, that wasn't the case. Ah, hell! I released my hands and dropped: my legs buckled under me and I rolled trying to dissipate the newly acquired kinetic energy—rolling like a parachutist—but I don't think it worked. My poor, already-wounded legs hurt something fierce as I limped down hill toward the tree line.

Reaching the cover of the trees—my breathing labored— I turned back to see where I'd been. There in the moonlight, was a towering medieval castle. The stone walls were at least forty feet high with tower structures pilastered along the walls to defend the outside. The battlements were pierced with loopholes for shooting arrows, and the overhanging battlements had holes in the floor for dropping hot oil on attacking troops. Kings were very serious about defending their castles. I could see the one small window way up above where I had just come from. I watched as the casement window was cranked shut.

I felt alone and abandoned.

I pushed on into the dark woods. What did he think I could do? "Take care of Erika," he said, but I didn't know if I would ever see her again. I'd no idea what had happened to her. And he said, "you must find her." How did he know I didn't know where she was? Why didn't he come with me?

And why was he smiling? Something wasn't right. At one point Wagner said they had his equation, then he said they needed him for the *rest* of the equation. Was he confused? It was me that was confused. And he called me Brandon Noble when he saw me. How the devil did he know my name?

Birds suddenly fluttered into the air. I stopped in my tracks and listened.

A rustle of leaves, I tripped, the ground came up to meet my face. I rolled over to find a shiny suit of medieval armor looming over me with a drawn sword. It was the suit of armor that stood in Fouquet's foyer, but now it seemed to have an occupant.

The armor took a step forward and the sword came swooshing toward me. I rolled out of the way and the blade hit an exposed tree root. I rolled back the other way as the sword sliced at the ground. It was only a dream, I was sure of it, just a dream. Wake up. WAKE UP! I slithered backward and got behind a tree trunk. The blade hit near my hand; bark exploded. I tried to peek around the trunk to locate this nightmarish vision. I moved left. The vision moved left. I moved right. The vison moved right. If this was a bad arcade game, I didn't want to drop any more quarters in the slot.

The glinting blade streaked toward me.

I ducked just in time.

I circled the tree trying to stay opposite this knight who was determined to take me out. I wanted to turn him off, pull the plug. Where was the on-off switch? I reached for a string of vines on the ground hoping they weren't poison ivy—leaves with three points?—I couldn't tell—hell, I pulled on the vine: the knight's feet became entangled and tried to pull his feet free. I pulled back a tree limb and released it; it hit him in the helmet. He came at me as I backed away from the tree, but fell forward, his feet still caught in the vines, his own heavy armor overpowering him. I kicked at his head, at his stomach. That only hurt my toes. He pushed with his arms to raise himself up off the ground. I just watched as he tried clumsily to get to his feet. I reached for his wrist with both hands trying to take away his sword. I squeezed, I wrenched, I pulled—the sword came free and I took it by the handle. The knight clamored to his feet and lunged at me. The sword sliced into the crook of his right arm; the arm went limp. I pulled back on the sword and tried to go for his left arm, but he fell toward me and the sword slid into his stomach just below his chest plate and burst out his back. His eyes went hollow and dead. The intimidating suit of armor fell back on its heels and crashed to the ground and the faceplate dropped open. The flesh on the knight's wretched face began to look flushed, pink, and then very pink and sunburned, then a third-degree red, and finally it went to a blistering hot white. His skin texture seemed to melt away and smolder. A putrid offensive odor stung at my nose, a smell like burning plastic. The man in the hammered steel began to dissolve and his fingers curled inward, his whole body curling up like burning oak leaves. All detail disappeared; his face melted away. Just red-hot armor plate now lay on the ground, a shell without a mollusk.

I stood there in total disbelief—and mortified. What had just friggin' happened?

An ugly burnt mass of wires and plastic lay inert on the forest floor, a few small flames re-igniting from the extreme heat. I bent down to take a closer look. A plastic toy thrown into a fireplace; that's what it looked like, just bigger; an ugly ball of—was that once a man? Or was this indeed an arcade game, or a dream? Was this some kind of cruel joke? Fouquet and his fascination for the medieval era—what new brew had he concocted? Artificial knights in shining armor? For what purpose? An amusement attraction? Who controlled this thing? Montford Fouquet? Was it some kind of automated guard? Did some kind of high-tech armor short circuit and kill the man inside it? The sword was still stuck in the melted mass that once was a—I didn't know what. The stench was awful—pungent and irritating. I had to turn away. The ozone smelled of burning electronics, burning plastic, and singed flesh—I couldn't tell which, maybe all and something else. Black, acrid smoke rose into the trees and a god-awful stench made me want to puke. I looked back at the castle looming in the darkness, and then turned into the woods.

twenty three

DAY FIVE. Saturday, April 5th. In my ragged clothing, with my scratched and bruised body, aching legs, and a stick for a cane, I headed straight for the police station. A ride on a dung wagon eventually got me to the *Heidelberg Polizei Hauptquartier*, an unimposing building of concrete block placed at the edge of Old Heidelberg. The sun was up now and I felt a little better—like coming out of a long dark tunnel. I brushed my matted hair away from my face; I had had a bad hair night… and I had had enough. Where had the police been while I was getting chased, beaten up, strapped in a dunking stool, poked with syringes, and attacked by a Medieval knight in electric armor? Weren't they supposed to follow me or had they stopped to choke down a few donuts?

I climbed, I limped, I crawled up the steep concrete steps to a pair of glass doors. The station was no different than what one might find in a small American city. To me it was a safe haven on the one hand, but just inside, was the wrath of God. The Inspector would not be pleased to see me.

"*Scheisse*! I haven't seen cyclone like you in long friggin' while," barked Inspector Schultz. "You've managed to turn my town upside down."

"I've got..."

"Sit your carcass down."

Well, at least I was in his office, not the interrogation room. That, I hoped, meant something.

The inspector crossed over to his side of the desk and with a gnawed-on pencil in his hand (I saw it as a lethal weapon) flipped open a manila folder. He had finally calmed down, I thought, until he vehemently shoved a stack of black and white photos at me; some went airborne and hit the floor. I picked up the one that landed in my lap: a photo of a car wreck—my white Bug and the black Mercedes. I looked at the other photos still on the desk: a panel truck, charred black and totally demolished, and a bloody, mangled human being crushed between a steering wheel and a broken car seat. Shards of glass were visible everywhere. The vehicles looked like crumpled tin cans, and the truck driver—charcoal grilled.

"Doesn't bode well for those racing along mountain roads with hairpin turns," I said.

"How fast were you going?"

"They were chasing me, bent on killing me."

"*Halt die klappe!*" He kicked my chair. "Enough! You're funny man, Mr. Noble."—He *was* still fuming—"Why everybody trying to kill you?"

"A medieval knight tried to kill me."

"A knight?

"And it wasn't human."

"What wasn't human?"

"The knight."

"You've been watching too many American movies."

"It tried to kill me."

"Calm down before I have to get you a straight jacket. You belong in sanitarium. You're a lunatic, Mr. Noble! *Verrückter*, lunatic!"

"I've lost Erika."

"You get her killed too?"

"She was with me in my VW."

"More, Mr. Noble, tell me more."

"I had gone to Strasbourg to see Dr. Fouquet and took Erika with me."

"There's your friggin' mistake."

"These ugly, deformed creatures attacked us…"

"*Sheisse!* You full of crap as Christmas goose. God help me, what's wrong with you, boy?" asked Gerhard as he turned to the window, no idea how to continue. How in the devil do you interrogate a nut case? That's surely what he thought I was.

"Where's Erika now?" he attempted finally.

"That's what I was trying to tell you, I frankly don't know, I was hit from behind…"

"Another car hit you?"

"No Inspector, someone hit me over the head."

"Is this before, or after, you destroy three vehicles and were attacked by, how you say, deformed creatures!"

"I get the feeling you don't believe me."

"Ha!"

"After the accident, Erika and I were walking down the road, tending to our wounds when…"

"Tending to what? *Auf jemanden scharf sein.* You got the candy ass for this girl, don't you?"

"If you mean…"

"*Spitz.* You're spending too much time with that girl."

"That's none of your…"

"Everything's my business. You got dead people all around you. That make you my business,"—Inspector Schultz paused to light a half-smoked cigar—"I don't know what to do with you, Mr. Noble. Jailing you could cause an international incident."

"I think you've got an international incident already."

"How so?"

"A large research laboratory, a secret lab around here."

"Researching what?"

"Professor Wagner is there."

Schultz leaned forward. "*Now* you're telling me something I want to hear."

"He's at a castle near Eberbach."

"The Schloss Hirschhorn?"

"I don't know…"

"You don't know nothing, you never know nothing…"

"I saw 'EBERBACH' on a road sign when I hitched a ride back here last night. He's there, I talked to him."

"Professor Wagner?"

"Yes, isn't that who we're talking about?"

"Blast, you're trying my patience, Mr. Noble."

He knew who I was; he knew my name! He'd never seen me before."

"Maybe he saw you on television…in Berlin."

"Maybe."

"I don't know where your head's at, Noble." The inspector opened his desk drawer and pulled out my camera and tossed it at me. "Did you lose something?"

"Thanks," I said, "that's my livelihood."

"Your livelihood! *Der Lügnebaron*, you're a baron of lies. I took the liberty of processing the film in your camera: a photo of our radio cars in front of Wagner's home, and three shots of a car wreck—yours—and well, nothing else!" The inspector held the filmstrip in front of my face. "Thirty six frames, all black—unexposed—except for those four. You take lot of pictures for a photographer."

"New roll," I said matter-of-factly.

Schultz looked at me with disgust, "Someone must have crapped in your brain and forgot to stir it. But far be it for me to delve into your private life, *Herr* Brandon Noble. Get up! Come with me. Maybe you can help. That would be something wouldn't it?"

Gerhard Schultz led me out of the front of the Police Station. A crowd had gathered across the street in the *Marktplatz*. I figured I must have really stirred up a hornet's nest, but then I saw that it was a political rally—they weren't here to string *me* up. A well-dressed man stood on a makeshift platform holding a megaphone. He was rattling off Germanspiel so fast I couldn't pick up a single word, but the crowd seemed to agree with what he was advocating. Banners and posters flew over the crowd, and the man at the podium looked real familiar to me, but I couldn't place him.

"What's he running for?" I asked the Inspector.

"Chancellor of Germany. He's Helmut Schmidt. Running on crime-fighting platform, he want safer streets. If he gets elected, I'll be out of job."

"You're doing your best, Inspector."

"*Danke*, Noble. It's so comforting to hear that from you."

We rode out to the crash site—my crash site—in the Inspector's shiny little blue Beetle. I was amazed at all the gadgets he had stuffed into that tiny vehicle. He had bolted or screwed or clipped to the dashboard, a short-wave radio, a clipboard, a radar gun, and sundry other gadgets. There was no room in the back seat to carry a prisoner though; they would have to bring the "paddy wagon" to pick him up. Earlier, I had given the inspector a rundown on everything that had happened to me as a pretty nurse—a very pretty nurse—cleaned me up at the Heidelberg *Krankenhaus*, the local hospital. I think, for some extra attention, I pointed out places on my body that weren't really injured. I didn't know I had so many wounds, but I did know I ached all over. I felt like I had been in a boxing match *between* two furious boxers. A couple of painkillers and foam wrappings on my legs would allow me to keep going, but where to? Where was I going? That I didn't know.

We pulled up to the accident site. A tow truck was pulling the black Mercedes out of the mangled mess. The area up the road was taped off.

"You walked up this way didn't you?" asked the Inspector.

"Yeah," I replied.

"We found blood on the roadway. Do you mind explaining to me how it got here?"

"We did find a few drops of blood."

"I thought it might be yours."

"Not mine. It must have been Tanovic's blood…"

"The Yugoslavian?"

"Yes, the lunkhead I was chasing in Berlin."

"That doesn't answer my question, Mr. Noble. How did *his* blood get *here*?"

"He fell out of the Mercedes."

"He what?"

"Well, I hit him with a crescent wrench."

"*Scheisse!* You're friggin' something you know that."

"What's that supposed to mean?"

"You're first-class nutball, that's what!"

"Oh."

"We found more blood over here beside the road," added the Inspector, "around these mashed up weeds. And we found drag marks on the road. There was a scuffle here and someone—weighing maybe fifty kilograms—was dragged off this way.

"Erika. Could it be Erika? Tanovic must have survived the fall from the Mercedez, and then hiding in the woods, he must have hit me and knocked me out."

The inspector pulled a plastic bag from his coat pocket—in it a piece of red material. "Is this what she was wearing?"

"God, yes. Her red skirt, and I don't think it was torn in the accident. Jesus!"

"You can't see it very well, but there's dried blood on this material," added Schultz, holding it up to my face.

"I...I remember, I think, I remember seeing a black-haired woman."

"Erika's is a reddish-brown..."

"I know, I saw a different woman with black hair standing over me."

"When did you see *her*?"

"It was like in a dream, and then later I saw her at the castle, behind a window, I think."

"You think?"

"The black-haired woman, *she* must have found me here and taken me to the castle...to Fouquet."

Just then a policeman ran up, "Inspector, our men are ready."

"Come with me, Mr. Noble," said Schultz.

"Where are we going?"

"We found another piece of Erika's skirt in the woods. We think we know where she is."

With a team of heavily armed policemen, we headed up into the woods. We could see matted-down brush; it was obvious someone had come through the woods recently. Another piece of Erika's skirt was found hanging on a thorny bush. I was trying to prepare myself for the worst. It was my fault. I had screwed the pooch once again. Erika was no ordinary woman; I knew that. So many things had drawn me to her: her beauty, her elegance, the way she walked, her absolute perfection. God could not have created a finer female to inhabit the earth—and with me, there could be another generation of them. But she was likely lost to me now, and it was all my fault.

We came upon a clearing. The police ducked down. A thatched-roof farmhouse built of half-timbered construction lay before us. It was a huge barn on a raised stone foundation. At ground level were the stables, and above them, the living quarters placed in the middle of this three-story barn-like structure. This arrangement protected the family from the harsh winters. But no family was stirring, and no chickens and no cows. The farmstead appeared to be abandoned.

The cops spread out to flank the farmhouse, communicating with hand signals so elegant that the maneuver could have been synced to ballet music. A squeaking sound suddenly broke the silence. Everyone ducked into the weeds. A window in the gable end of the barn banged shut. Just a breeze, we thought, and everyone breathed a sigh of relief. The cop next to me raised slowly up to take another look—

BANG! SPLAT!

His face was blown clean off.

I stood up screaming, "Christ, I can't take this anymore." I jumped up and down as if I had been standing in a fire-ant bed; my skin was crawling and it wasn't with ants. Every muscle in my body had pulled tight. I couldn't get my body to stop shaking. I was freaking out! The inspector pulled me to the ground and tried to hold me down. My face and clothes were spattered with blood. "I can't friggin' take this anymore. I just put on clean clothes. Crap!" I heard shots fired at the house and stood up trying to see what was happening. The inspector pulled me back down.

"There, in that second-story window," I yelled, "I see that stupid, grinning asshole."

"Calm down, Mr. Noble! You're loosing it."

"That's him, that's Tanovic," I yelled, "there's only one way to take down that son of a bitch: kick him in the balls!"

"We'll get him, Mr. Noble. It's our job."

"The hell, you say. That scumbag will get you and all your men—and then he'll get me!"

"Calm to hell, down!" thundered Gerhard Schultz.

This was finally too much for me. Vietnam hadn't cornered the market on horror. We got a war right here in the streets. Where's that freedom we've been fighting for when mothers have to walk their kids to the bus stop, and be there when they return? This wasn't *Leave It to Beaver* anymore. The inspector was right, he was absolutely right. The first thing about freedom is feeling safe, being safe, and being able to carry on with your lives without constant worry. That's what we pay our governments so much money to do: police, fire, and secure our goddamn borders. That's right, secure our goddamn borders! Our government had failed us. Idiot liberals too busy spending our money on barrels of pork. One could build a crap load of houses with all the pork barrel projects—

"Move in," motioned one of the policemen as they advanced toward the building.

"You stay here," said the Inspector as he raised up and dashed for the farmhouse. I watched as cops carefully approached the house from both sides.

I didn't have to go to Nam. I was lucky enough to get stationed right here in Germany—at Campbell Barracks— U.S. Army Europe, two-hour shifts, standing at the gate to the compound checking the ID's of everyone that entered, day and night. And guard duty walking a fence line at three A.M. in the morning. Freezing weather, ankle-deep snow, and frozen toes, just to protect an abandoned ammunition dump.Sometimes we carried an empty rifle; we couldn't be trusted with a loaded weapon, too many G.I.'s high on hashish. I was an MP—a military policeman—in a unit of the Headquarters Company. I pulled guard detail at the stockade or picked up a drunk GI from a *Biergarten*. It was a boring, routine job until the Baeder-Meinhoff Gang went on a rampage. We had to tighten security and search every car for bombs. The terrorists had been using car bombs to blow up businesses and military installations. I had no idea what their beef was; I just did my job—

On the opposite side of the clearing, just beyond the farmhouse, a blue Renault drove up and two men jumped out. They were reinforcements, but they weren't ours: they started taking pot shots at *us* and the police found themselves in the middle of crossfire. Guns cracked in all directions. Tanovic appeared through an upper window again, bandaged, bruised, and a crooked smile on his face. He raised his shotgun and fired down at the men below. If I had a gun, I thought, I could pick him off from here. I just needed a gun. A gun can solve a lot of problems. I decided I needed to solve this one; I was determined to move in myself. Erika was in there, in danger—if not from Tanovic, then from the wild firefight. I picked up the dead cop's pistol, a Walther PPK. This was it; now was my chance; the bad guys were busy with the police. I ran to a window at the side of the house and smashed the glass and climbed in. A bullet report and the window frame over my head blew away, wood chips showering down on me. I dropped to the floor and took in the room: a living room with a flower-patterned couch, a large television in a dark mahogany cabinet, a handmade breakfast table with highly ornamental legs— probably from the Black Forest region of Germany—a long scalloped coat rack screwed to the wall by the kitchen door with heavy coats and hats, and a nice Persian rug with a complex pattern of flowers and vines in muted colors on a polished birchwood floor—

The front door banged open and a policeman entered, rifle at the ready. He raised it to shoot at me and then realized who I was. A shot rang out; he jerked backward and fell back out the door and slid slowly to the ground leaving a trail of blood on the wall behind him. In his chest was left a bloody gaping wound from the tumbling bullet.

I peeked out the front window. The inspector was shooting at one of the men from the Renault. A bullet hit its mark. The man jerked. His head twitched, rapidly jerking back and forth like a man overdosed on hard drugs. His arms shook violently. Life, if there ever was any, left him.

He began to glow red and loose body detail. The flesh of his body smoked like battery acid and dripped off his skeletal structure. He, it, the thing, finally fell over and curled up. The inspector was stunned at what he had just seen; he stood frozen in his tracks, disbelieving. The thing melted to the ground into a glob, little flames flaring up like cooling magma. Another shot rang out and the inspector spun around—a violent bee sting—he was shot in the left arm. I could hear him yell German expletives: *Der Schweinwhund! Verdammt noch mal!*

I crossed the room on my knees and pushed open a door. The room was devoid of the person I was looking for. The dining room was empty, the kitchen empty, and over the sink a broken window. I decided to take the narrow service stairs to the second floor. With my every deliberate step, the stair treads insisted on creaking loudly. I halted at each step, and listened, Walther PPK at the ready. 7.65mm Browning ammo, one shot would do it. Who would I find first, Tanovic or Erika? Was I prepared for either one? I didn't think so.

At the top of the stairs, I took the first door to the right. Grabbing the door handle, I pushed. I heard a moan. The door creaked open. Dust curled off the floor. Erika was there, laying face up on an old iron bed with a bare mattress. Her hands and feet were tied to the bed frame and her clothes were torn—blouse and skirt ripped, underwear showing. Completely vulnerable. Her mouth gagged—her sweet, inviting, sumptuous lips parted with a tightly wrapped strip of red cloth from her own skirt. I rushed to her. Her beautiful chestnut eyes looked deep into mine.

I untied her and we embraced—a long embrace—the rest of the world vanished.

A stair tread squeaked.

I froze.

And another squeaked.

I gripped my pistol tightly.

The door swung open. The floorboards exploded in front of me. For a moment the boom deafened me. Time cranked itself down to a near standstill. Wood chips fluttered in slow motion back to the floor, each reflecting a glint of light from the dormer window. A haze of dust particles softened the image. As I watched, a wood chip somersaulted slowly to the…"Brandon!"…I awoke from my stupefying trance and pulled Erika over the back of the bed. A second blast blew the plaster wall above me into cement dust. Pieces of a framed picture and strips of wallpaper showered down upon us.

From under the bed, I could see Tanovic's feet: he wore *American* GI combat boots, the best name in military footwear, but badly scuffed up; they needed a polish. I pulled the trigger on my PPK. Black boot leather, and a couple of toes, went flying to the heavens. His roar of agony scared the crap out of me, but I composed myself and raised up for the parting shot, but Tanovic had his double-barreled shotgun aimed squarely at my face. He had the drop on me and he cracked that "crap-eating" grin of his. His head and chest were wrapped in white bandages, looking like a mummy from an Egyptian tomb come to make good on an evil curse. I had screwed up for the last time. I had made that final mistake.

He pulled the trigger.

I heard a click.

And nothing happened. He hadn't reloaded. I was still in this world.

My turn.

I squeezed the trigger on my weapon.

It fired—

But the bullet only grazed his shoulder, lucky me. I could only hope he'd come down with lead poisoning…fast! I jumped up and kicked to his groin, but I hit something hard. Tanovic didn't flinch; he didn't keel over in pain like he had done twice before. He just snickered and said, "cup."

Hell! He was wearing a jock strap with a hard plastic cup, like football players use. He found his weak spot and did something about it. He wasn't as dumb as I thought. I took a deep breath and had no choice but to throw all my weight at him.

I pushed Branko Tanovic backward and he crashed through the second-story window.

A long moment later, I heard a dull thud.

I looked out the window. There, lying sprawled in a grotesquely twisted manner, was the burly Yugoslavian; he no longer had that crap-eating smirk on his face.

The firefight had died down outside. I pulled Erika up from behind the bed. She seemed strong and unshaken, having taken all this, all to well. She was doing much better than I was, that was for damn sure.

"Are you all right?" I asked.

"I'm fine, and you?"

"Great. *Now* I'm great."

"That's good," she said with a strong, endearing smile.

"He...he didn't do anything to you...did he...I mean..."

"Oh, no—I'm fine, and did he do anything to you?"

"For the last time. But, Erika, I found your father...I saw him."

"He's okay?"

"He's fine, just fine."

"Is he outside?"

"No, I'm sorry, he's not here. But I told the police where he could be found. They'll get him back."

I led her out of the attic room, but two powerful hands from nowhere wrapped themselves around my neck. My Adam's apple was turning to sauce, my windpipe collapsing like a bent straw. I uttered only a frightening wheeze. Erika tried her best to push him off me. She kicked at his shins, threw cute little punches but they only aggravated him, just as a pesky mosquito would. He pushed her away, then brought up a gun with his other hand and pressed the muzzle into my loin. I felt helpless. I had forgotten about him, the other man that had come in the blue Renault. His face was expressionless and he looked familiar to me, hauntingly familiar. Had I seen him at the castle?

"*HALT! FRIEREN!*" came a piercing command from downstairs.

The Renault flunky turned toward the stairs and got off a shot before a bullet screamed into his left temple and, on the way out, blew off the right side of his face. Hollow points made a mess of anything they went through. A fireworks display ignited in the hollow of his head. Smoke streamed from around lifeless eyeballs. His skin began to crawl. He was becoming very hot to the touch and I tried to wrench myself from his grip. The boiling skin dissolved around the hair on his arms. Pulleys and cables and electrical circuitry were exposed as the skin dribbled from his body. I contorted my body, he fell over onto me, and as his carcass began to crumble around me, we both tumbled head over heels down the stairway leaving behind a trail of metal and electronic parts. Sticky, burning goo oozed down the steps. For a faint moment, I saw Erika standing motionless at the top of the stairs, seeming very far away. I peeled the smoldering, mangled plastic from my body and burned the flesh of my palms in the process. Then I felt something beside me and craned my neck to look—

Inspector Schultz lay sprawled out beside me staring at the ceiling, his hands clinching his neck, blood oozing out between his fingers. His orange sunglasses lay broken on the floor.

I brought my face close to his. "Hold on Inspector."

"What have I just seen?" he whispered, choking on his own blood, a gob of deep red life flowing from the side of his mouth.

"Hold on. The medic will be here any minute."

"You, you…"

"I know Inspector…this was all my fault. You told me to back off and I didn't. Next time I'll look before I leap. That's a promise."

"You can't change, Noble…it's in your blood."

I tried to raise his head up to help stop his choking.

"Noble."

"Yes?"

"Be true to yourself."

"I'll get them Inspector."

"You can't save the world, you're not up to it. Leave the criminals for someone else to…"

On that, he choked, and closed his eyes. He could no longer see the world he had spent so much time in. But maybe it wasn't a world he was looking forward to seeing.

"*Herr* Noble," came a voice, "You and Erika come with me. Our medic is here now to help Schultz. If you two are okay, we'll take you home."

That was fine by me. I was exhausted.

twenty four

ERIKA squirted some greenish-looking gel on the palm of her hand. She spread it ever so delicately with the tip of her fingers.

"It doesn't look too bad. Please take your shirt off."

"What?"

"Let me look at your back."

I pulled my wool sweater and shirt off in one move, but caught them on my wrists, my hands confined as if in a straight jacket.

"Turn over; lay on your stomach."

I pulled on the sleeves, but they would not release themselves.

"Lay down," Erika demanded.

I obliged—my arms tucked under my chest.

"Ooh, this looks pretty bad, your shoulder is all black and blue."

"It's okay, it'll be fine," I said.

"I have an emollient that may help. A nourishing moisturizer, it'll rehydrate and soften your skin," said Erika as she warmed the silky cream in the palms of her hands and spread it with her long slender fingers, touching me ever so tenderly.

"*Bactine*, that's all I nee…"

"This is much better. It's got Extracts of Sage and Rosemary and Witch Hazel and Dandelion petals…"

"Hush!" I said.

She worked the moisturizer slowly into my wounds, but her hands gradually took on a wider circle, reaching my neck and temples.

"Does that feel good?"

"Oh, yes."

"Where else do you hurt? Here?" Her gentle hands slowly circled down my back and then she put a hand on my still clothed buttocks—my pulse quickened.

"Could you turn over please?" I turned over. She looked at me sweetly, her chestnut eyes beckoning. Her pink lips, moist and full, drew me to her. Her silky auburn hair fell from her shoulder and brushed my face. My heart beat faster.

"I love you," I said. It just came involuntarily, but I felt I meant it. I felt bliss with her. This moment must never end, I thought.

She kissed the corner of my mouth and then pulled back. I ached with anticipation.

Erika began to unbutton her blouse, ever so slowly, her pretty white neck opening itself to me. Another button was eased out of its buttonhole, revealing voluminous mounds of flesh. They called out for me, her cavernous cleavage drawing me in. I wanted to pull the silky blouse aside to reveal her wonderments fully, but my hands were still constrained by my shirtsleeves.

She moved lower and unbuttoned my pants and grabbed the zipper and pulled down on it. I ached with pain, and it wasn't my wounds I was feeling.

Her breasts beckoned, but her black lacy bra held them firmly in place. I wanted those voluptuous mounds set free. I wanted to caress her splendid, shapely frame. I wanted my hands tracing her tiny waist, her firm thighs, and her supple behind. I wanted to run *my* fingers across every inch of her throbbing, feverish body.

I looked into her glimmering eyes: they were burning with passion. She kissed me just above my manhood and then ran her tongue across my belly. I trembled. She raised my arms over her head and came up to me and kissed me sweetly on the lips.

We lay on a large, plush velvet sofa in the middle of the drawing room of her father's house and all I could feel was her flesh pressing against mine. She smothered me in sweet love.

twenty five

DAY SIX. **Sunday, April 6th.** Warm, life-giving light filtered through the loosely woven shear curtains hanging over the narrow, ceiling-high windows. They filled the room with soft, caressing light. I looked over at Erika still asleep in her luxurious bed. A feather-down comforter enveloped us and Erika sighed a moan of peaceful bliss. I looked at her supple skin, her seductive lips, and her soft flowing hair. Her back was bare, white, and without imperfections. Her spine peeked through in perfect alignment. I eased out from beneath the covers and wrapped myself in a sheet.

When she awoke, I had a tray of breakfast treats for her—a poached egg, aromatic strips of crispy bacon, and a plate of Belgian waffles dripping with syrup and covered with fresh fruit. A steaming hot cup of coffee and a glass of thick, ice-cold orange juice completed the sumptuous breakfast. She didn't know it, but I had gone down to the café on the corner to get it; I was no cook, just check the cupboard in my apartment.

"How wonderful!" she gleamed as she sat up in the bed, exposing her perfectly formed breasts and hard nipples.

I melted like ice on a hot summer day.

"Put the breakfast over there, honey…and come to me," she cooed as she threw aside the covers, revealing her glistening essence.

I tore off my clothes and dove back into the covers.

It was late morning, very late, and I scanned the hundreds of books in Professor Wagner's library: *Mathematical Methods in Quantum Mechanics, Symmetry Principles In Solid State and Molecular Physics*—an unbelievable fifteen-hundred pages—and *The Theory and Application of Hyperbolic Systems of Quasilinear Equations*—I was exhausted just reading the titles. And all in small print, no wonder scientists wore bottle-thick glasses. In these volumes were technical and scientific terminology and mind-boggling mathematical equations on every page. I figured an advanced civilization from another galaxy would even have a hard time digesting this stuff.

"Your father must be real smart," I laughed.

"Uh-huh." Erika approached me and handed me a cup of hot tea. She hugged me tightly around the waist. "He's a genius."

"That smart huh!"

"I. Q. one-eighty-six point four."

"I don't know what mine is."

"You're more than enough for me."

"My I. Q. or my…"

She grinned at me.

"I need to look around some more," I said. "Anything that would tell me more about your father."

"Sure."

I pulled a box—what could best be described as a plain black metal box—off the shelf. It had a toggle switch and voltage meter and two short power cords, one with a DINN plug, the other with a European two-pin plug.

"Erika, do you know what this is?"

"No," she replied in a dull monotone, "but they're everywhere."

"I noticed. There's several in your dad's laboratory…and one in your bedroom on the bedside table."

"Yes, they've been lying around the house a long time, but I have no idea what they're for."

"Then why don't you…"—Erika bent over to look in a lower cabinet and that's when I, uh, lost my concentration. Her beautiful rosy cheeks peeked through her sheer emerald-blue nightgown. The window's back lighting revealed her long, slender, perfectly formed legs—and the long space between her thighs as it ran all the way up to her—

"Honey."

"YES!" I replied.

"Here are some *Phillips* cassettes that…"

"Music, sure, play something…"

"No, these are father's recordings, they have music labels on them, but they're not music…"

"Let me see those! Where can I play them?"

"Over there in that cabinet."

I slipped a cassette into the player and pressed PLAY. Wagner's voice came forth: *"Tape 23, session sixteen, speech notes, Annual A. I. Symposium. Humanoid robots, real in almost every way, are made possible by the new biophysics. Gentleman, with a new understanding of the relationship between molecular structures and electron flow, we've perfected the Electroplasmic Brain. Not chemical synaptic activity, but electron transmission and cross concurrence that's capable of simulating the subtlest of human emotion with absolute control of all synthesized neurological functions. By using human ova and hormone control, an epidermal layer of human flesh is grown over a skeletal framework of porous synthetic resins, thus totally defying external examination. It is the perfec..."*

I hit the stop button and turned to Erika. "Did you know this was what your father was working on?"

"Working on?"

"He calls it the Electroplasmic Brain—synthetic gray matter as it were—to be put in an artificial body."

"I don't understand."

"You don't know what an android is?"

"Android, an automaton made to resemble a human being."

"That's right. A machine designed to operate automatically in response to instructions previously fed to it."

"But, human-like, that's just science fiction," Erika added.

"Uh-huh. And it couldn't really think for itself. It wouldn't be able to handle the real world of unexpected situations."

"I see. How are your bruises? Shall I rub some more cream on them?"

"Don't *you* have any bruises *I* can rub that lovely cream on?"

"No."

"After that beating you took from Tanovic?"

"No, I rub cream on you."

"Sure, my love, you can." Androids could wait. We returned to the bedroom where the breakfast tray still lay on the bedside table, the food uneaten.

twenty six

S IT MR. NOBLE."

I sat down on the plush velvet sofa in the drawing room, my knees together, my back straight, my shoulders square. I cradled a hot cup of tea in my hands that Professor Wagner had just given me. He sat down on a heavily upholstered and tufted armchair opposite me—and stared at me intently. I thought, if only he knew what I had done with Erika on this very couch—

"You're sleeping with my daughter, aren't you, Mr. Noble?"

My jaw dropped. I stared back at him, unable to respond.

"That's fine, I don't need to know. You come here and want to have little fun—I understand."

"But sir," I said, "that's not what…"

"She's a magnificent creature, you think not?"

"No, I mean yes," my teacup rattled in my hands, "I mean, she is—definitely."

"Is she not, how you say *belohnung*—rewarding?"

"Rewarding?" I shifted in my seat uncomfortably.

Just then Erika walked into the room completely nude, no blouse, no skirt, not a stitch of clothing. She seemed unaware, or unconcerned, that she was wearing absolutely nothing, standing there naked in front of her father. What would Professor Wagner think now? I was embarrassed beyond belief. Erika walked over to me and handed me the diapered baby. He looked so like me, but had Erika's pretty chestnut eyes. I held the baby up to my face, my arms outstretched in front of me. The baby stared at me as if trying to figure out who I was.

"I am yours," the baby said. The baby's mouth had moved.

"You're my Papa. Let's play. Let's do the Ferris wheel. Turn me upside down."

The baby was talking to me—he could talk! And he was only a few months old.

"I am a magnificent creature. You are my Papa…"

Sunlight streaked across my face. A bright light was burning through my eyelids. I found myself in Erika's big bed. I must have dozed off. A dream, a terrifying dream, I tried to remember the details, it was quickly fading from consciousness, returning to that netherworld from which it came. The images were disturbing; I felt uneasy. Where was Erika?

I got up and traced through the house. She wasn't there. Maybe she had gone shopping or something. Women do that…when they're happy, and when they're sad. Any excuse is enough for them to go on a shopping spree.

The phone rang, and rang, and rang as I looked around to find it. I finally found it stashed in an empty kitchen cupboard.

"Hello?"

"Is that you Noble?" The voice was muffled and distorted.

"What? Who is this?"

"It's me, Inspector Schultz."

"Inspector? Inspector Schultz? You're still with the living?"

"I not calling from grave."

"I'm not so sure...I can't believe..."

"The Plastic People haven't gotten me yet."

"That's good," I said.

"I'm at Krankenhaus Heidelberg."

"I'll be there shortly," I replied and cleaned up and hopped a tram to the hospital.

The Inspector had his arm wrapped in bandages, an oxygen line stuck in his nose, a wire taped to his finger, I-V's in both arms, a plastic feeding tube stuck in his belly, and EKG discs taped all over his bare chest.

"Just a flesh wound," he said as I tried to hide the revulsion appearing on my face as I entered his wire strewn hospital room. Several monitors beeped, each with a different sound.

"Yeah right, shot in the arm *and* the neck!"

"Missed the carotid artery by a kilometer."

"Lucky you."

"Lucky me. *Glücklich tag*."

"And your arm?"

"I'll regain full use of it in a month or two," said Schultz. "No bones were shattered."

"Christ, I'm glad to know you're not all fucked-up."

"*Nicht verstehen?*"

"Don't got your ass on backwards."

"*Was?*"

"You believe me now?"

"I do, but I don't know what it is I saw...ow..."

"Don't try to talk now," I insisted.

"Good friggin' thing it missed my larynx."

"Good thing—but no yelling for a while, you hear?"

The inspector squirmed in his bed. "You got a cigar?"

"You kidding me!"

"*Nein*. You can smuggle one in, easy."

"Sure, right."

"I want one last smoke before those friggin' Plastic People come to get me," said Schultz.

"Yeah."

"I thought you were full of crap—something big you said."

"Something big, all right."

"What do you think is goin' on?"

"I found a tape at Erika's. Professor Wagner talks about a Electroplasmic Brain to be fitted into an android's head—for superior artificial intelligence he says."

"Androids?"

"That's right. Artificial machines to simulate humans."

"Get me that friggin' cigar!"

I stood at the *Strassenbahn-Haltestelle* in the *Marktplatz* waiting for a tram to Schwetzingen when a sporty cherry-red hatchback—a beautiful Citroën with a powerful V6 Maserati engine—pulled up beside me. The passenger window lowered itself slowly.

"Brandon Noble, care for a romp?" came the voice of a doll. I was flabbergasted.

"A ride I mean…I mean I need to talk with you."

She was the lady with the jet-black mane. I leaned down into the window, "I saw you at the castle," I said. "And I know it was you who hit me over the head."

"Oh sorry, dear, I explain it to you, come, get in."

What could she want? Was I about to be abducted again? If by her, well, that didn't seem such a bad thing. Besides, I could find out more about her—and the castle. If there was any trouble, I figured I could take care of myself.

So I hopped in.

The red coupe peeled away from the curb.

My eyes were on her beautiful profile—not the Citroën's, *her* shapely profile. Her silky black hair fell neatly over her forehead to just above her eyes; it had the deep sheen of a newly polished car. The hairdo was short, but not sassy short, it curled neatly at her shoulders. Her black eyelashes, unnaturally long I thought, probably add-ons, didn't stop me from following the ski-slope curve of her nose, a very dignified nose, strong and determined. Her tiny mouth wore a dull burgundy lipstick, like a dark antique rose. I sorely wanted to kiss it—ever so softly and sweetly.

My eyes drifted across her bare shoulders, obscured only by narrow spaghetti straps that held up a flowing black silk blouse—a blouse that formed nicely to her perky breasts. She wore a white pearl necklace tightly around her neck and a very short, mini-skirt. I could see the ends of the garter belt straps holding up her shear black stockings leaving her upper thighs bare—they were tight, firm, and healthy looking.

"You know Erika do you not?" she asked.

"Yeah?" My attention was shifted back to what the mysterious woman had to say.

You taking good care of her?" she asked with a strange smile.

"I only just met her," I replied.

"Well, it's time you meet me. She's not the only pretty girl in town."

After she finished throwing the shifter into third, she reached over and touched my hand ever so delicately. An old lady scampered across the street; her direction zigzagged like a scared rabbit's as she tried to determine the track of our nimble sports car. Our dust engulfed a wagon driver who swerved off the road and dropped his load of hay.

"You speak English so well…"

"Well, thank you, you're so sweet."

"Erika speaks flawless English," I said, "well, except for conversational phrases…"

"Enough about her, sweetie, my name's Dominique, and

you are a very handsome man. From America it looks to me. They build great men in America. You've got great buns."

I didn't know how to answer that, but I think I blushed a bit.

"I detect an accent in your very good English," I said," but I don't think it's German."

"You're so good, Noble. You're right, of course, I'm not German. I'm too pretty to be German, don't you think? I shave my legs."

"Uh, yes, you do. You look cosmopolitan, a lady of the world."

"But I must be from somewhere?"

"Uh, I don't want to guess."

"Come on. *"Un beau morceau, vous je veux."*

"You're French!"

"I am."

"What did you say in French?"

"Oh, sweetie, you don't want to know, maybe later I tell you."

We turned onto the Autobahn and then she really opened up; I mean the car, the car opened up. A hundred-ninety clicks. The tach was close to redlining. Dominique's hair blew wildly when she opened her window; she looked as if she was trying to live life *now*, right now, and for all it was worth. She didn't come across as the arrogant type—the snooty kind I saw peering through the window at the lab. This woman was a free spirit. But I didn't know her intentions, well, until she pulled my hand to her stocking and then up to her bare thigh—

And then she eased my hand toward her crotch.

I felt her velvety skin, soft and without imperfections, but I...I pulled back and returned my hand to its proper place, in *my* lap—at least for now.

But *her* hand stayed on her white thighs, and it slowly ran north, her titillating fingers racing along the insides of her thighs as her eyes remained fixed on the road ahead. Her hand slipped further upward, pulling her black mini upward with it. I too tried to look straight ahead, but my eyes wouldn't obey.

Her lips parted. I could sense a moaning from deep within her. My member began to ache.

I moved my hand back to her thigh and pulled on her hand. In the process, I saw that she was wearing no panties and her cute bush was wet.

"Pull over. Get off this friggin' autobahn!" I screamed.

She looked at me and smiled, "Why sure sweetie."

The Citroën screeched to a stop near a large haystack. I quickly jumped out.

"A romp in the hay?" she asked.

"No, you stay in your car Miss…Miss Dominique."

A vexation of spirit fell over her face—a failed conquest? But she didn't give up: "Come sweetie, come get back in the car, please; you won't be disappointed. I'll take you to a nice discotheque. We can dance all night."

"Thank you, that's a fine offer," I said as sweat beaded on my forehead. "Another time maybe."

"Okay sweetie, it's your loss."

She slid her shifter into first gear, gunned the engine, let out the clutch and squealed the tires, leaving me standing in a puff of acrid smoke.

"I have no doubt," I replied.

twenty seven

DOMINIQUE intrigued me; she was about as forward and uninhibited as any woman could be, in
fact, only in a man's hotest dreams. I returned
to reality, to Erika's cozy, safe abode. I was sure of her, no
mystery about that woman. I found her in a white bathrobe
curled up on a plush couch watching television, her hair
still wet from a hot shower. I knew she was wearing nothing
under that robe, and my mind was fixed on that thought as
I sat down beside her.

"Inspector Schultz is going to be fine," I said.

"That's good."

She was engrossed in an afternoon soap opera. I noticed
that the show's characters revealed much more skin than in
U.S. soaps, lots of boobs and butts and overt sensual bedroom romps. American prudes would be outraged; American censors would have a baby. Maybe that's why Erika
seemed so open, so warm about our relationship; her *society*
was more open about sex. They have fun with it; even the
commercials are edgy and shocking. I really didn't know
Erika that well and yet we seemed like symbiotic beings—
as if we had been together all our lives. I pulled her robe
open so that I could see her cleavage. She didn't seem to
notice—or mind. She was the girl of my dreams, of all men's
dreams I suppose. But, for once, *I* had her.

A news flash cut into the soap: *"We interrupt this program
to bring you this developing story. We're going to take you live
to the scene. Adelfa Willmann is there now. Adelfa."*

"Yes, Dimitri, we're outside Schloss Hirschorn am Neckar,

nine kilometers west of Eberbach, where a unit of the special police has broken onto the grounds and secured the perimeter. Sources tell us they believe this is where Professor Wilhelm Wagner is being held hostage. . ."

A whole host of blue cop cars were scattered across the middle ward just beyond the moat. A drawbridge led to the outer gate, which was flanked by two round towers. The drawbridge was in the down position—probably hadn't been up in centuries—and the ominous iron gate, with its huge skewering points on the bottom, was up, but the heavy timber doors were closed tight as an oil drum.

I sat up. "They're going in! That's where your father is."

"Then we must go."

"Go where?"

"To the castle."

"We can't do anything there."

"We can be there when they get him out."

Erika bounded out of the room, I assumed to get dressed, not my preference. I looked back at the screen. Policemen were brandishing automatic weapons and wearing defensive gear—helmets, bullet shields, cumbersome bulletproof vests—and advancing quickly on the castle. It didn't look like a place we should go. Two men threw grappling hooks over the outer wall. An attack team looked to be setting explosives in front of the doors to the gatehouse. They then ran back across the drawbridge. Moments later, the doors were a shower of splinters. The TV camera shook. It looked like a full military assault. Men climbed the ropes to breech the outer curtain wall. A team advanced across the drawbridge and ran through the outer gatehouse. Gunfire popped all around. The reporters were screaming in their microphones as they hid behind their broadcasting trucks—

"I'm ready!" Erika returned, dressed up nicely in so short a time.

"I don't have a car."

"You can use my father's car, here's the keys." She threw them at me.

The doctor's car was in the carriage house: a shiny emerald-green Mercedes, a 280SL convertible! Now it seemed I had it all.

twenty eight

D RIVING the Mercedes was a thrill, but this was no time for a Sunday drive. Erika was determined to see her dad. We drove up to the Hirschhorn castle, but were halted at the police security line. We told a corporal who we were: I was a photographer from *die Bild-Zeitung*, that meant nothing to him, but when I pointed to Erika, he got on his walkie-talkie.

The shock wave from an explosion shook our car.

I turned to her, "I think we should go back home. This is no place for us."

"My father's here."

"Let me take you back down the hill to a café. I can come and get you when it's over."

"I want to be here when they bring him out."

A gray uniform approached the car. "You have Erika Wagner?" asked a police sergeant in full riot gear.

"Yes," I said.

"*Verzeihung*, Miss Wagner, sorry, we haven't found your father yet. We've got men inside now, searching every chamber in the castle."

"Have you run into a lot of resistance, Sergeant?"

"You the American, Brandon Noble?"

"Yes."

"The Inspector told me to ask you what happened to the cigar he requested."

"I inten…"

"And he told me to keep an eye on you."

"Just one eye?"

"I won't be as nice to you as the Inspector. I intend to watch you carefully, Mister."

"Any resistance?"

"Uh, actually no. Our only resistance is from three-hundred-year-old doors and Neckar Valley stone."

"No *army* of resistance? No guards in Medieval armor?"

"No. But we're on the lookout for Schultz's Plastic People." He chuckled as he said this.

"They're for real, Sergeant, believe me."

"*Eine Schdraube locker haben?*"

Erika laughed. The sergeant looked at me with a crooked condescending grin. I didn't understand what he said, but I was sure he wasn't being nice.

"See any men in white lab coats?" I asked.

"I thought maybe you'd seen some in nut house?"

"Not a one, and you? Seen any in this castle?"

"Not a one."

"This can't be right. There were a lot of people here the other day. Did you find the basement laboratories?"

"Nothing so far." The Sergeant stood up and removed his cap and scratched his head, clichéd as it was. "I don't understand it."

"Maybe they heard you were coming," I said.

"Maybe."

"Maybe you got the wrong castle."

"The wrong castle! Wagner was *here*, that's what *you* told the Inspector."

"I didn't tell him he was *here*, at *this* castle…"

"Does this look like the castle you were at?"

"Well, not from this side, I left the back of the castle in a forest of trees."

"Trees! Where? There are no trees on this scraggly rock."

"That's what I'm talking about, this *isn't* the castle…"

"Hirschhorn, you said Hirschhorn, Hirschhorn on the Neckar."

"No, I didn't Sergeant, I told the Inspector I saw a sign, Eberbach."

"We're near Eberbach; it's just nine kilometers further up river!"

"It was dark Sergeant, I'm not sure this was…are there any other castles in the area?"

"*Ja*, but we've already checked those out."

"Not by blowing them up, I hope."

A stern look came over his face. "*Hirschhorn am Neckar*, this *must* be the castle." The sergeant walked away mumbling, "The Inspector will send me to salt mines."

I turned to Erika. "Your father is not here. They've been all over the castle."

"He's not here?"

"No, I'll take you home now."

twenty nine

ON THE way home that afternoon, the road took an "S" curve across the railroad tracks. A bright green 2CV Citroën approached, one of those low-end Citroëns built by the French to replace the donkey cart. It was a great little car designed to navigate rough dirt roads and cobblestone streets and it could make its way easily through a farmer's plowed field without breaking a load of eggs because of its soft springs. The Germans call it *"die Ente"*, The Duck, because of its off road abilities and its duck-like waddle as the body sways loosely on its chassis.

The 2CV was moving too fast and it wasn't going to make the turn. I jerked the Mercedes off the road trying to give it room. Everything seemed to shift into slow motion. The 2CV's rear wheels broke loose, and it went airborne and looked like a hard-boiled egg rolling up on its pointed end, and then it dropped down again. It seemed so surreal. The car rocked to a stop on the railroad tracks. I was stunned. It seemed like a dream.

"Brandon!" Erika shook me to reality.

I looked through the front windshield of the Mercedes. In the signal tower, the gatekeeper stood up and motioned for our attention. I looked back at the 2CV lying on its side: no one had climbed out of it.

"Come on!" I jumped out of the car and ran for the wreck. Erika followed. I looked down into the front passenger window. "I don't see anyone. There's no one here!"

"Here he is." said Erika, "He's in the back seat." Sure enough, the driver was there curled up in the back, and he appeared dazed. I opened the passenger door and reached in and pulled him out. He was loopy and seemed unaware of his situation. Then we heard banging on the tower window: the gatekeeper was screaming, about to have a coronary. He was waving his arms frantically. I finally understood: a train was barrcling down on us and we were still on the tracks. The worst scenario flashed through my mind: I could see the train hitting the 2CV at eighty miles an hour, pushing the tin box for miles until it exploded into shrapnel. I could see the gatekeeper with his first black mark in his forty year career. These gates could have been electronically controlled, tripped by the train, but this was a socialist country, and everyone was given a job. Even with modern high-speed trains, these traffic gates were manually operated—

"Come on!" I yelled.

Erika and I lifted the car back on its wheels; I was amazed at the ease with which we did it.

We pushed on the front bumper of the 2CV.

"Push," I said, "push!"

Erika pushed. The 2CV jumped easily over one rail and then over the other. I think she could have pushed it off all by herself. I heard the rails humming and felt the ground shaking. The 2CV rolled away from the tracks and *Scheeeeew*, the train raced past us and was gone in seconds. Einstein's train, I thought, traveling close to the speed of light.

Time slowly wound back down to its normal speed. I looked up at the gate tower; the keeper had sat back down and was mopping the sweat off his brow.

"That was exciting," said Erika.

"Uh-huh, right," I replied. She was so calm about it.

"Where's the man we pulled from the car?" Erika asked as she looked in every direction.

"I don't know." He was nowhere to be seen.

"He must have wandered off."

Or was this all a dream? I wasn't sure. I needed a *Heineken* or two, maybe three. No maybe it was time for schnapps.

thirty

I WALKED into the bedroom and saw Erika's dress thrown on the bed. A bedside table lamp projected a ring of light on the ceiling and a warm glow on the bedcovers. Sitting on the vanity was a black-haired Japanese porcelain doll with a red silk kimono and umbrella. It had a child strapped to its back and it had big round eyes like a child's. Music played on Erika's little Hi-Fi, I think it was a

Burt Bacharach song, *I'll Never Fall in Love Again*. American music had become popular in Germany and it wasn't just Elvis and the Beach Boys: Led Zeppelin and The Who where there too.

I could hear the shower running so I wandered on into the bathroom, and this really was a *bath*room: just a bath, no toilet; the toilet and the bidet were in another room. Steam began to fill the room. Several lit candles threw shadows pulsating on the ceiling. The lightly frosted shower curtain was the only thing between Erika and myself. I could just make out her figure, a soft-gray curvaceous outline. She was washing her hair, scrubbing it, giving it a workout. I hoped she wouldn't mangle it, take out all that red color and natural vitality. Her breasts fell so perfectly, looked so firm, as did her exquisite behind. My eyes meandered down the silhouette of her legs—

"Brandon?"

I came out of my trance. "Uh, yeah, it's me, just…"

"Come on in baby."

"I…I'm still dressed…"

Without warning, a dripping wet hand grabbed my wrist and pulled me in.

"My clothes!" The water drenched my shirt—and quickly soaked my pants. She kissed me hard on the lips, then slowly unbuttoned my shirt and sensually ran her fingers over my bared chest, over the tuffs of hair on my muscular torso. She wrenched the shirt down off my arms.

"Um, I love your muscles; you're so strong." She squeezed on my biceps; I tensed them hoping to impress her. "My!" she said, and then ran her eyes slowly down the rest of my body. "Oh, you've got your shoes on."

"I said I was still…you didn't give me time to undre…"

"Oh, poor dear. Get them off now, before you step on my toes."

Before I could remove them, she was unzipping my pants.

Gallons of water saturated my corduroy slacks, and soon that water would be all over the tile floor. She grabbed me around the head and kissed me again. My hands found her slender waist, felt the curves as they widened downward. She was all curves, from her nose to her breasts to her waist to the back of her thighs. I ached as I traced my fngers over all of them. Water beaded up on her skin, and then ran softly away, revealing every pore on her lovely body. I licked her. Her skin trembled. She licked me. I exploded with pleasure. Her plump, heaving breasts pressed against my chest. Her legs found there way around mine, entwining tightly—we were one.

Before long we wallowed lazily in the tub, bubbles frothing over, wine glasses clinking, and a Bacharach piano playing *Close To You,* and *What The World Needs Now Is Love.* She knew them all by name, every Bacharach song—and she knew all the lyrics. We caressed each other until we wrinkled up like California prunes, and then the candles went out.

thirty one

DAY SEVEN. **Monday, April 7th.** Once again, I found myself in Erika's bed as the morning sun glared into the bedroom. I wondered how my apartment was doing. The rats were probably having the time of their lives—bread crumbs, unwashed dishes—and then Professor Wagner came to my mind. Where was he? He wasn't at the *Hirschhorn am Neckar,* wrong castle, but there were hundreds of castles in Germany. At which one was he?"

I would have to leave Erika for awhile and see what I could find out, go by the newspaper office, check on my apartment. I said *auf Wiedersehen!* to Erika and told her I would return that evening. She said she'd be waiting, all sweet, beautiful—and naked.

I hopped the tram to Heidelberg. That was to be my transportation until I could find another bargain-priced vehicle. Don't get me wrong, the tram wasn't a bad way to get around. The tracks went almost everywhere within the city and its outskirts, and went to neighboring towns like Schwetzingen. You really didn't need a car and the station waits were very short.

Three minutes later I was cruising through the suburbs in the tram. I thought about the equation on the burnt piece of computer paper. It was the key to what someone wanted—badly. Printed out on computer paper. Computer paper? That's it! Where was the computer? A computer main frame takes a huge amount of space. Maybe at the University of Heidelberg? They might have one, and that's where I might find out more about Professor Wagner or come up with a useful lead. I got off at *Zwingerstrasse* and climbed the steps to the administration building. This was the oldest University in German, founded way back in 1386.

"Yes, sir."

"I'm looking for Professor Wilhelm Wagner. Does he teach here?"

"Wilhelm Wagner, just a moment please." She left the counter and went to a vertical file, a nice old oak one, not like the steel cabinets at *die Bild-Zeitung*. She flipped through the file, "T—V—W, hum, no, he's never taught here."

"Sure?"

"Yes, and no special speaking engagements."

"You sure?"

"Yes."

"Do you have a computer here?"

"Computer? Ah, yes the LARC."

"The LARC?"

"From Sperry-Rand."

"Takes up a huge room doesn't it?"

"Yes, in the basement, the whole floor is raised up to run all the massive cables between the various components. And the room must be kept a certain—cold—temperature. I wear a sweater to go in there."

"Does it have any output devices—that print out data—*outside* the University?"

"Outside the University, why heavens no, they're all near the computer room."

The likelihood of another computer in this city was, well, unlikely. Maybe there had been one at Sunstone Laboratories, but it was now burnt toast. Main-frame computers were much too expensive even for large companies and they required hordes of programmers and support personnel and a lot of paying users. Even *die Bild-Zeitung* didn't have access to one. It then hit me that these monster computers would require a lot of electricity to run. And who would know who was using a lot of electricity? The electric company, of course. This was not an industrial or manufacturing town, this should be easy, I thought.

I beat it to Elektriztät Heidelberg and they were happy to give me a list of their biggest customers: Krankenhaus Heidelberg, Die Dunkelalters gmbH, Kurpfälzisches Museum and the University of Heidelberg—I had been there. I needed only to run down the rest and see how they were using that power.

After a few phone calls and searches in surrounding areas of Heidelberg, in Frankfurt, and in Strasbourg, there were no other computers to be found. Could Professor Wagner be using the University's computer without them knowing, under an assumed name perhaps?

I went back to see the Inspector in the hospital, to take him a Cuban cigar.

"About time, *Herr* Noble. The thanks I get for keeping you out of Clink."

"Sorry, inspector. But you can't smoke in here."

"I go on roof. They got elevator to roof garden, staff go there to eat lunch—and smoke. Nurse!"

Gerhard Schultz pressed on his emergency button on the wall with one hand, the cigar clutched in the other, and his neck wrapped in bandages so thick, his head looked like the point of a ballpoint pen.

"Nurse! Bring me wheelchair."

The nurse put the Inspector in a wheelchair and I pushed along his I-V pole.

On the roof, we found a shady spot under an awning and set out a chessboard on a concrete table. I got the black pieces and so he got to go first; he tried the Fool's Gambit, but I broke that plan up with ease. It was going to take a lot longer for him to beat me.

"You meet Colombo?" asked the Inspector.

"Me, no, he lives in California."

"I like Colombo, good police detective."

"He's on television…"

"He fool the murderers. They think he's a stupid busybody; don't know nothing, but he see everything, forget nothing. He good detective, smokes good cigars."

"But Inspector, he's just an actor. He's not a detective."

"He good, get his man."

"Are *you* going to find Wagner and get *his* kidnapper?"

"I find him." He moved a knight out from behind his row of pawns. His move put my queen in danger. I took his knight out with a lowly pawn and spared my queen.

I told the Inspector I had run down electrical usage, having seen the computer paper in Wagner's lab and he was impressed, well, until I told him the afternoon netted a dead end.

"Maybe Fouquet left country with Professor Wagner, to France," said Schultz.

"No, Dr. Fouquet—and the Professor—are in a castle around here somewhere—somewhere close."

"We think Branko Tanovic and Jake Finger were in the employ of a company called Die Dunkelalters, a large machining company."

"Die Dunkelalters! They're one of the companies that uses a lot of electricity, and you know, come to think of it, Fouquet told me he owned a company that builds industrial computer systems in the States. That couldn't be a coincidence."

"What's the name of this company in States?"

"PLCS, uh, Programmable Logic Control Systems."

"You know what *die Dunkelalters* means?" asks Schultz.

"No."

"The Dark Ages."

"Sounds like a beer."

"No, the Medieval period in our history."

"Ah, see there, Inspector, I'm not *Verrückter*!—I'm not crazy. And Fouquet said he also had a plastics factory in the States."

"Plastics for Plastic People."

"Fouquet is planning to manufacture a lot more androids."

Schultz moved his King's rook in position to threaten one of my bishops. I moved my bishop out of harms way and he took out one of my pawns.

"Just a pawn," he said, "of no import."

thirty two

I RETURNED to my apartment and climbed the four flights of stairs. As I started to put the key in the lock, I heard my television. I didn't think I had left it on. I was then hit with a flashback of Fouquet's wine cellar and the TV blasting upstairs. I carefully inserted the key, quietly grabbed the doorknob, and turned. The door inched open. My eyes shot around the room. My apartment was in a mess: dirty clothes lay on the floor and the dishes were caked with food; it all looked quite unhealthy. My well-organized and routine life had taken a turn. The television blared with a soap opera. Suddenly, a dark figure—having been hidden by the back of the couch—stood up and turned toward me.

"Hi sweetie!"

It was Dominique. I was relieved and terrified at the same time. She stood there in a short pleated skirt—but she wore no top. Her bared breasts stood firm before me.

"You have a nice apartment," she said.

"Apartment, no, not in the lea—" I was focused on her breasts as she took a few steps around the room. "What's this?" she asked.

"Uh—a Murphy bed," I replied just barely able to speak.

"A bed!" She grabbed the ring and pulled down on it and out came the bed. She plopped down on it, her legs spread, her skirt revealing more that it should. My body tensed up.

"Do you like what you see?"

I was speechless. What was this woman doing to me? Dominique sat up on the edge of the bed and began to undo my waist belt.

"Am I better than she is?" Dominique asked sweetly as she put my hand on her breast. I pulled it back.

"You don't have to answer now, darling." She stood up from the bed. "I have so many more wonderful things to show you."

"I'm sure you do."

She pushed me down on the bed and climbed on top of me. There was no resisting her.

I'm sure the Murphy bed shook the apartment below. The television flickered, throwing dancing shadows on the evening wall—

After we had thrown some shadows of our own, I sat up in bed wiping the sweat from my forehead. Dominique looked over at me with an approving smile.

"How you feeling, honey?" asked Dominique.

"Great."

"Was it everything you imagined?"

"And then some."

"I'm pleased."

She got up and slipped on her skirt, then her blouse, and finally her black high heels. She must not own any undergarments, I thought. Which was fine by me.

"Sweetie," she said. "Did you know Erika was my sister?"

My insides froze. "Your sister?"

"Yes, dear." She blew me a kiss as she hurried out the door, closing it gently behind her—her beautiful hips the last thing I saw, well until I looked out the window and saw her get into her red Citroën. She quickly zoomed off, the engine revving to the redline before she reached second gear.

I popped open a *Heineken* and slumped down on my sagging couch in front of the TV. I put my feet on the Ottoman—well it was just a wooden crate, but it performed the same function.

Sister? Erika's sister? Why would she tell me that? Was it true? Dominique was French, not German, at least I thought so, but how do you really know? Erika said she could speak six languages. And Dominique, who knows how many she could speak? But their accents should give them away, shouldn't they? Did these two divas know each other, worse, know what each other was doing? My God, if they did, there was something very scary and unnatural about them.

I took a big swig of my cold beer. Was Dominique just a sex kitten? Was I just a hot lover to her? Was I an afternoon fling to satisfy her beastly yearnings? And why would she go out of her way to tell me she was Erika's sister? Just a little SNAFU in my search for the truth. I guzzled down the rest of my *Heineken*.

My head went to spinning. If Dominique *was* Erika's sister, she too would be Wagner's daughter. Or maybe just the reverse? Both Fouquet's daughters? I didn't know what to believe anymore and maybe that was the idea. Dominique was just toying with me. Erika, her sister? No way, they were nothing alike. Well, they *were* both alluringly beautiful.

I opened another *Heineken*.

The evening news was coming on, my daily fix of current events. There was famine in the Middle East and Congress threatened to impeach President Nixon; the Watergate scandal was turning Washington upside down. Bravo! Tricky Dick had drafted me—with a lottery no less, with a game of chance—and I lost. Two years in the Army, but I was lucky, extremely lucky; they sent me to Germany instead of Nam. The war was winding down and it was only a matter of time before we tucked in our tails and skipped town. Congress had already changed the name of our unit, but it was still there. Simply by changing names, Congress could say to the public that they were downsizing the military. They published a long list of units that were decommissioned, but we—and many of the others—were still there;

just the names were changed. We had to redesign our unit patch and make new company stationary, but our mission stayed the same. Go figure.

I looked at *die Bild-Zeitung*. A marijuana drug bust had gone bad; a cop and two teens were killed. A baby fell into an ice chest at a public picnic and no one noticed—it quietly froze to death. And a man was refilling his lawnmower with gasoline in his garage, and it exploded. Is life—and death—already in the cards? Life is transient. Do we have any control over our fates? Elfie Detrich didn't. I wanted to be in control. People die because of something they did, not because of a bad roll of the dice; I tried to convince myself of that. They just made a last mistake. But how many mistakes are we allowed to make before our last—

A report blared on the tube about a thief in Bertchtesgaden who had been quickly picked up by the police after robbing a house in his own neighborhood. How did they find him so quickly? Walking home, the idiot had left his tracks in the snow. Most criminals are stupid, I guess, if they weren't they wouldn't be criminals—

The political news covered the upcoming 1974 popular elections for members to the *Bundestag*, the first house of parliament. Currently, Chancellor Willy Brandt and the Social Democratic party controlled it, but a new coalition with the Free Democratic Party was giving the minister of finance, Helmut Schmidt, a good chance of becoming chancellor, the chief political executive in the German government. Would it change anything in government policy? I doubted it. I was feeling pretty good; no one had tried to kill me lately.

I popped open another *Heineken.*

thirty three

DAY EIGHT. **Tuesday, April 8th**. Glass blew out of the windows. A fireball of flames rushed toward me. I dived for cover and covered my head. Moments passed and I heard the fire crackling. I heard alarms going off. I heard glass and metal crashing to the ground. I lifted my head and peeked. Another explosion engulfed the building in flames and black smoke rose into the sky. It was the Sunstone Laboratories building, two-stories once wrapped in glass, now just a stack of cement-block pigeonholes. I could see furniture and chairs and filing cabinets sitting on the concrete floor spans. It looked like the back of a giant dollhouse. Papers fluttered through the air. Little pops—explosions—deep within the building, broke the otherwise serene appearance of the scene. A large black & white photograph floated into view. Four scientists in white lab coats stood there looking at me, their eyes all on *me*. Suddenly, they all began to laugh—hardy, roaring laughs. They pointed; they were laughing at *me*! I felt like a horse's ass. Professor Wagner broke into a big grin—

I turned over and set quickly up in bed. My eyes came into focus. I had been dreaming again and it was very unsettling—nightmarish to say the least. Stress, I thought, too much stress, too much going on in my life. I wiped my eyes and brushed my hair from my face. Where was I? Not my bed in the States, my twin bed by the window with the sheer curtains my mother had put there many years before, now ragged and faded. No, I was in my apartment in Heidelberg, far from Buffalo. I felt like a fish out of water. I was confused, alone in my apartment, and alone in the world. I was tired—exhausted mentally and physically. Erika, Dominique, Erika, Dominique, Professor Wagner, Dr. Fouquet, Dr. Stravinsky, Dr. Stewart, to many doctors—my head was swimming and I hadn't had a *Heineken* since last night, maybe *too many* last night. I tried to focus on the Ottoman and saw dead soldiers: one bottle, two bottles, three, four, five—crap! I dropped my head back on the pillow. I knew one thing, I was going back to Erika's—well, as soon as the apartment stopped moving. Maybe she could give me something soothing for my throbbing head.

thirty four

WHEN I got to Erika's, I found her putting nail polish on her toes. She didn't ask why I hadn't come back that evening. I was uncomfortable and just played along with her unconcern for my long absence. She didn't ask any questions, not even about her father. I didn't volunteer any answers; I didn't have any. What would I have said, "I just slept with another woman last night"?

"Brandon, could you get me a brush, a hair brush in the bathroom, I want to brush my hair."

"Oh sure." I was now second banana. She had slipped into another world—and it wasn't mine. She seemed distant, like a long lens zooming out to a wide-angle—tunnel vision.

"Erika, how about you and I go for a walk down in Old Heidelberg, see what we can discover. I'd like to see the old church, hike up to *Schloss Heidelberg*, do a little shopping?"

Erika perked up, "Sure, I'd love to."

I had finally gotten her attention.

It was now Tuesday afternoon and Erika and I meandered past a Baker's Shop filled with confections—rolls, bread, cakes, and fritters—the sweet aroma wafting from the open door. Erika pulled away from me and rushed in. I stood outside watching her through the glass windows. She looked so lovely and effervescent. This day she was wearing a short charcoal-colored pleated skirt and a gray cardigan sweater over a lacy white blouse. Her legs were covered with black stockings and she wore brown, leather-laced, high-top boots. I had never spent so much time looking at women's clothing until I met Erika—of course it wasn't really the clothes I was looking at. She filled out those clothes so perfectly—so deliciously. And she moved in them so alluringly.

Erika soon dashed out of the store with a smile that went from ear to ear.

"Here," she said as she firmly handed me a confection wrapped in waxed tissue paper.

"*Dunke.*"

"*Bitte schön.* Go on, open it."

I unwrapped it. It was a creamy butter-cream cake. I took a big mouth-watering bite; half of it remained on my face.

Erika laughed, "It looks good on you."

"I bet."

"You bet what?"

"It's an expression."

"More slang?"

"Yes, I suppose."

"What does it mean?"

I shrugged my shoulders.

"And I confuse you!"

I then noticed that Erika wasn't eating any of the confection. "Erika, aren't you going to have some?"

"Oh no, it's too sweet, and bad for my figure."

"But...you were smiling like a Cheshire cat when you came out the door..."

"I got it for *you*."

"Oooh-kay. So what can I get for you?"

"Well…I'll think of something."

And I figured she would. She was a bit strange. I can't say I understood a thing about this girl. Something wasn't right. Sure she was foreign to me, a German, with German culture under her belt. How could I be expected to understand where she was coming from in so short a time.

"Erika…do you…well, what plans do you have for the future? I mean, what do you like to do? Do you plan to keep living at your father's house? You know…"

"We have to find father first—then maybe—have you heard from the police yet?"

"I talked to the Inspector yesterday at the hospital, we played a game of chess, I lost. He's doing well. He asked me if *I* had any new leads. Mine were dead ends. Tanovic and Jake Finger work for Die Dunkelalters; ever heard of them?"

"No."

"Dr. Fouquet may own it. It's a machine shop."

"What do they make?"

"I'm sure it's parts for the Plastic People, the androids. Fouquet is up to no good."

Erika stopped in her tracks and peered into a display window—it was a sex shop with weird-looking paraphernalia displayed wall-to-wall in the huge picture windows opening onto the street—there for everyone to see, including children, including me. I tried not to notice, but Erika, she had to stop and look. She seemed fascinated by the contraptions.

"My, what's that for?" Erika asked.

I blushed, I had known of such things, some of them, but had never seen them first hand. I was flabbergasted. It was clear, Europeans weren't inhibited in the least, but I hoped Erika wouldn't want to go inside, at least not bring me in there. I was embarrassed enough as it was, and going inside with a beautiful girl, oh, man! We American men had a lot to learn; we had a lot of inhibitions to throw aside so we could really have some fun—

Erika went into the sex shop, but thank God, she didn't pull me in with her. I stayed outside, waiting with my hands in my pockets, peeking at the strange paraphernalia—wondering how some of it was used—and hoping no one on the street saw me ogle the merchandise. It was definitely embarrassing, standing there looking in.

Suddenly a squeal of tires, I turned.

A red sporty Citroën drove up beside me, *the* red Citroën. It was Dominique. I knelt down to say hello to her.

My jaw dropped. She wore only a tank top. That's all, nothing covered her below her waist—well except the red stilettoes on her feet. Her bare bottom snuggled against the black leather seat, her beautiful legs feeling free and uninhibited, ready to wrap around and squeeze anything that might get within their grasp.

"Hello, Brandon, need a ride?"

My heart stopped. I glanced back to the sex shop and then returned my gaze to the black-haired seductress. "No thanks, Dominique, I've got business to take care of. I can get the tram just around the corner. I'll be fine…"

"The tram doesn't have concubines."

My jaw fell all the way off.

She eased her legs apart.

My libido raced. And it wasn't just my heart that was throbbing. My God, she was hot. The leather seat was getting wet—and Erika was just inside the sex shop.

"Sorry, Dominique, I really…"

"*Vous m'êtes très sympthique.*"

"What?"

"I'm crazy about…" Her voice trailed off. Dominique's cheery smile suddenly turned to a frown.

I stood up.

Erika had stepped out of the sex shop and Dominique squealed off in her red Citroën.

"Who was that?" Erika asked.

"Just someone asking for directions."

"To where?"

"Uh, the Heidelberg Schloss."

"I see. Oh, here, this is for you…for us."

Erika handed me something in a long slender box. I turned red and then tried to change the subject. "It looks like the kids are all into hip American things, bell-bottom jeans, page-boy hairdos and…"

"That's right."

We came upon a street show. Marionettes danced in a makeshift puppet theatre with dozens of children sitting cross-legged in front of it.

"They're doing *Romeo and Juliet*," Erika said excitedly.

"Is that Juliet?" I asked. "The pretty lady that looks a lot like you."

Erika cooed and took my arms in hers. "And Romeo looks like you, my darling. Let's go home."

"Okay," I said. I was beginning to feel like a puppet on a string, completely beyond my own control. "But it's still early, don't you want…"

"We could go to the discotheque."

My heart missed a beat. "The discotheque?"

"They play your American music, rock and roll, disco, Donna Summer, The Village People."

"And you like Burt Bacharach?"

I stopped and looked at a handbill on a power pole advertising an Eric Clapton concert, and below that a bill promoting a Vietnam demonstration in Bonn. Vietnam—it seemed so far off now.

"Brandon? Are you okay?" asked Erika. "You seem distant."

"Huh, Erica, what? Oh, the bill, it reminds me of who I really am: an MP who got someone killed."

"What?"

"It happened at Campbell Barracks. While inspecting a car at the compound gate, I failed to use this mirror-on-a-stick thing to check the underside of a car, and I sent the car on through. The car drove on into the quadrangle and stopped in front of Headquarters Company—

and boom!"—Erika stepped back—"The car, my car, blew sky high, shattering windows and blowing a big hole in the side of the building. There were numerous injuries and one man died. He was a friend of mine. I couldn't go home, back to States, after that, after my tour ended. You see, I couldn't face my family. I couldn't face *his* family. That's why I'm still here in Germany."

thirty five

WE RETURNED to Erika's pad—but she was no longer the only girl on my mind. This other woman was making me crazy, not love crazy, nuts crazy. Free and casy was an understatement. She was hot, very hot. I should never have slept with Dominique in my apartment, but she was definitely fun. I could just imagine the places she might want to *bumsen*: in the car, on the tram, in a phone booth—

"Brandon…"

I jumped.

"Here's your gift."

My mind was twisting.

"You said it was for both of us?"

"It is darling, open it!"

We were in the drawing room, sitting on the velvet couch now. Erika crossed her slender legs.

"Maybe you should open it," I delayed.

"Okay…you're such a prude." Erika ripped it open and held it up high for examination.

I blushed.

"Let's try it out," she said with the curiosity of a child.

"Does it need batteries?" I asked.

"Of course, it's a machine, it needs a power source—even if it's a device for giving pleasure."

Erika unscrewed the cap: it needed batteries.

Just then, the door of the Black Forest cuckoo clock on the opposite wall slammed open and the wooden bird began its nerve-racking *cuckoo, cuckoo, cuckoo*—

"The clock has batteries," said Erika with a sparkle.

"Cuckoo clocks don't have batteries," I said.

"This one does, I saw father putting them in."

I gave her a puzzling look and got up and lifted it off the wall, but it caught on something: an electrical wire was preventing me from bringing it more than a foot away from the wall. I looked at the back of the clock and removed a small tube about the size of a shotgun shell. There was glass on one end: a lens! This was a miniature video camera, or at least the optics. The electronics had to be somewhere else, I thought, no one can make a video camera this small. I looked apprehensively around the room. I picked up a porcelain figurine and then a Russian Fabergé egg; anything I thought could house a tiny camera. My mind was racing. I looked under a lampshade—and there, screwed between the socket and the bulb was another device: a tiny microphone. Someone was watching us—and listening.

I hurried into Erika's bedroom. There, on the dresser, the black-haired Japanese doll with big round eyes. One of the eyes glinted. I grabbed the doll and banged it against the edge of the dresser; the head shattered into chunks of porcelain; a small camera remained in my hand.

Erika entered the room, her bubbly smile disappearing when she saw the mess. "What have you done?"

"You see this? It's a video camera! A damn video camera! What do you know about it?"

"I don't know anything."

"Someone is watching us, don't you get it? Do you know where the video recorder might be?"

"Video recorder?"

"A tape machine to record what the camera sees."

"I…I don't underst…"

"We're gonna search the house now. Take me to every closet, nook and cranny."

"That sounds erotic."

"Ah, crap! Are you trying your hand at humor now? Come on."

We began our search of the house. I looked for hidden wires, I looked for false walls and hidden doors, I looked for hollowed out books and electrical devices, but found nothing except a couple more cameras and mikes, all with cables going directly into the walls. That meant the wiring probably ran through the attic.

"How do we get to the attic, Erika?"

"I don't know."

I was frustrated, not just with Erika, but I knew whoever was watching us, now knew we knew, unless the image was only recorded on tape and not transmitted—a real possibility, but not likely since the 2-inch tape machines would take up a lot of room and have to be monitored and loaded with new tape reels every few hours. So I figured someone had to be watching at this very moment. I looked for trap doors in closet ceilings, and doors in the paneled walls of the hallways. But nothing. It was like Erika's refrigerator, always empty. I was running out of options. I pulled on the drawer of a dining room sideboard and my eyes widened. Lying on top of a stack of placemats was a shiny silver pistol.

"Erika," I called to her, "Come here. What is this?"

I picked up the gun and turned toward her.

"Father's old gun. He was in the resistance in World War II. The Americans dropped thousands of those guns…for anyone willing to pick one up and fight the Nazi's."

"I've heard of them, they called it the *The Liberator*, a cheap tin gun made by the United States. Then your father was not a good loyal German?"

"What do you mean? He *was* a good German: he worked for the Fatherland on secret projects."

"There's too many secrets around here for my taste. Who the devil's watching us, Erika?"

Erika pushed up to me, wrapping her arms around me, hugging me tight. "You're so wonderful, Brandon."

"You don't know everything. I'm not the person you think…"

"You're so sweet. You're my darling."

I was feeling low, like a heel, like a scum-sucking bottom-feeder living in the deepest ocean depths. My stomach tightened.

"I have to tell you something. I…I love you. I've never felt like this about anyone."

Erika looked directly at me, waiting for more, her penetrating eyes fixed on mine.

"You've got to believe what I'm about to say."

"Believe what?" She took a step back, her lovely smile disappearing.

"Believe that it meant nothing."

"Our relationship means nothing?"

"No, I don't mean you."

"Not me! Then who?"

"Your sister!"

"My sister? I don't have a sister."

"Isn't Dominique your sister?"

"Dominique? I do know her; she's Dr. Fouquet's daughter."

"Then why did she go out of her way to tell me she was your sister?"

"I don't know."

"Fouquet's daughter, you say, well, she *was* in the castle with him."

"What did you do with her there?" asked Erika, with a curious expression.

"I...I didn't do anything there. I just saw her there, but..."

"But what?"

I grabbed her tenderly around the waist. "I slept with Dominique." There, I'd said it. Erika pulled away and stared at me with confused and hurt eyes.

"I'm sorry," I said.

"How could you? I'm the best." Erika turned away from me.

I approached her and touched her lightly on the shoulder.

She tensed up, pulled away, and repeated, "How could you? I'm the best."

"I don't know. I . . . I, I'm an idiot." I turned away. "It meant nothing—just a fling." I couldn't believe I had said that.

"Do I not have a perfect body? Great in every..."

"You're perfect. The most beautiful woman I've ever known."

"Then why?"

"I...I..."

"Just a fling, that's all. It tells me Dominique is better than I."

I turned back toward her. "No...she's not."

"Yes...she is. You proved that." Erika stepped close to me, her face changed, her demeanor suddenly shifted and a weird smile came across her face. "Let's have sex with our new toy."

"God, help me." I screamed in pain that came from deep within me.

She grabbed my crotch. I pulled away.

"Baby, don't you want to play?"

"No…yes…no, I mean no, not now. I've got to think." My head was swimming and it wasn't from *Heinekins*.

I made a beeline for the front door, her voice trailing behind me, "Brandon! Dominique only acted *à la fran-caise…*"

I slammed the door behind me.

thirty six

Á LA francaise, she said: like the French! What to hell does that mean? Dominique *was* French. I was confused and distraught as I wandered through the cobblestone streets of Schwetzingen. How could she be so trifling? Didn't she understand what I had said? I cared about her. Didn't she understand that? I didn't mean to hurt her. Boy, did I screw up.

I stopped in front of a Travel Office window with a display of posters and maps and objects collected from around the world. There was a "sand-carved" miniature of the Egyptian Sphinx, and a hot air balloon with vertical stripes in the colors of the rainbow and a white flag that read: AROUND THE WORLD IN EIGHT DAYS. Eight days! Yeah right. World-wind fun that would be. A large TV monitor was playing a tape about the local tours on the Rhine River. It showed the Lorelei, the legendary rock in the middle of the river, and told the story of the *Mäuseturn*, the Mouse Tower at Binger Loch. That's where, according to legend, Archbishop Hatto, a stone-hearted oppressor of the poor, did, after a hard winter, put an end to the complaining of his starving congregation because they were demanding access to his large personal stores of wheat and grain. He did so by inviting them into his barn to make repairs and in return for their work, he promised them food for the winter. When the barn was full of the "wretched beggars", as he called them, he barred the door and set the barn on fire. As the barn became engulfed in flames, he uttered aloud with a satisfying grin, "Listen to my mice squeaking." But before long a throng of rats came scurrying out of the barn and chased him to the Bingen Tower which was situated on an island in the middle of the Rhine River. He thought he would be safe there, but the rats devoured him—chewed him up unmercifully—gnawing at his flesh and picking at his bones. It was his Day of Judgement. At some point we'll all get there.

The tape also showcased the majestic medieval castles of the Rhine that stand precariously on their escarpments: the Gutenfells, the Stahleck, the Schloss Rheinstein. Rheinstein sat on the west bank of the river. That was it! The castle I had been taken to. Schloss Rheinstein! The wooded area, the battlements, that had to be it. It wasn't too far up the Rhine. I passed through there on my trip back from Koblenz through the Rhine Gorge. "Eberbach", the city sign I saw that night. The wrong Eberbach! I looked on the big colorful map of Germany hanging in the window and looked along the Rhine River above Heidelberg. There, sure enough, was another town with the same name, Eberbach, about eighty kilometers down river. I couldn't believe it; I had sent the police in the wrong direction. The Hirschhorn, and several other castles, are on the Neckar. The cops checked them all out—up river—but they didn't go down river on the *west* side of Heidelberg where the Neckar flows into the Rhine.

Damn! I had been on the opposite side of town from where I thought I was.

I turned and ran back down the street toward Erika's.

thirty seven

I RAN UP the steps and entered the Wagner home.
"ERIKA! I know where your father is. I found him! The right castle this time."

Erika came into the room with a sour expression on her face. "What do *you* want?"

"I know where your father is. Come on, get your coat, you're coming with me."

"You found my father?"

"I'm sure of it…but I need your help."

"Oh, Brandon. You're so nice."

"Yeah, right—enough—come with me. I'm going to get your father back to you if it takes…"

"Let's go."

thirty eight

THE RHINE was beautiful, the castles divine. She was divine. I told her my plan. We were in the 280SL on our way to Rheinstein and we had a plan to get into the castle. The Rhine valley was beautiful as always. Low clouds had settled over the mountain peaks and rays of sunlight moved across the deep green, vineyard-covered landscape. Erika began to talk—far more than I had ever heard her utter before. It was beautiful; I just listened.

She related to me the legendary story of the Lorelei, the rock outcropping in the middle of the Rhine River, or so I thought—

"She was beautiful and enchanting," began Erika. "Knights from all around came to court her. Every man that set his eyes on her became hopelessly in love."

"When did this happen?" I asked.

"In Medieval times. She lived just up the river from the rock near the village of Bacharach."

"Bacharach?" I said surprised. "And you like Burt's music! Is that a coincidence or what?"

"Or what, I just love his music."

"That's obvious. Just go on with your story."

"You see, Lorelei was her name—that's where the rock got its name—and she finally found true love in a young knight who, after promising his hand to Lorelei, went off to war and never returned. Other suitors came to her door, but the young knight was all she could think about and she spent years in tears praying for his return. But he never came."

"Aw," I said.

"You men, never romantic."

"Sorry, go on."

"Well, this beautiful maiden finally gave up after turning down many men in shining armor—men who went off to kill themselves because they couldn't have the enchanting Lorelei. Their deaths put tremendous stress on her and she decided she would have to leave her castle to hide from her suitors. She decided to go live in a convent."

"A convent? You're kidding?"

"Kidding?"

"Your pulling my leg, you're not serious?"

"I am serious; that's where she was going. But before

leaving, she wanted to take one last look at the castle of the young knight she so dearly longed for. She climbed a precipice overlooking the Rhine to look at the castle of her lost knight just across the river, and as she did so, she saw a sailing ship approaching a bend in the river, and there, on the bow of the ship, was her long lost love."

"Wow!" I said.

"Lorelei cried out in joy and waved her arms frantically. The boat crew saw her and was distracted by the bewitching maiden. The steersman forgot to guide the boat and it crashed into the rocks. The boat broke apart and began to sink. Lorelei screamed at her lover's peril and cried out his name, and, and…" Erika looked like she might cry.

"You okay?" I asked.

"I'm fine. Do you want to hear the rest of my story?"

"I do, I do!"

"Then listen…she jumped."

"She what?"

"She jumped—dove into the treacherous tides of the river to save her lover—and she was never seen again! But her singing is still heard echoing on the canyon walls at night."

"Her singing? I don't get it…"

"The ghost of the distressed maiden still stands on that rock in the middle of the river, singing mesmerizing songs that lure mariners to their death on the perilous rocks. Many ships have gone down there and they say it's because of the beautiful Lorelei."

"Aw."

"Brandon!"

"It's a good story," I said.

"It's not a story, it's true."

"Okay, if she's responsible for the deaths of so many sailors, how is that romantic?"

Raising her eyebrow, Erika viewed me the way women sometimes do when they're perturbed at something you said—with daggers in their eyes.

"You know a lot of legends and stories?" I asked.

"Uh…no, just this one."

"Just this one?"

"Uh-huh."

And Bacharach song lyrics, strange, I thought. She was cheerful and unaware of my puzzled expression. I figured she'd know all those romantic Rhine River legends. I looked at her, trying to see behind those mysterious, unrevealing eyes.

"Okay—Erika, we're almost there—I recognize the Mouse Tower over there on that island. I saw a video on it so I too have a Rhine River story to tell, but it's just four more clicks and we'll be there, at Schloss Rheinstein."

"Good."

We left the river road on the Rhine's western bank and drove up a steep hill. We passed a uniformed man working out of a plumber's truck and followed along a dirt road that wound around the hill and up through the woods. Approaching the outer gatehouse, we eased to a stop.

"How do I get in?" asked Erika.

"Come on, just do as I told you, they'll let you in. Your beauty will bewitch them; no red-blooded knight could resist. You drive, I'll hide in the back seat."

We drove on up to the castle gate as I hunkered down in the back. Erika, ever so delicately, exited the vehicle, her long sleek legs sliding from the leather seat as if she was a movie star emerging from her limousine on Oscar night and all eyes were on her. She walked up the drive, one foot in front of the other, hips swaying.

She pressed the gate bell next to a huge fifteen-foot-tall timber door that was still hanging on iron hinges forged centuries ago. A smaller six-foot personnel door opened within the larger one. A big man stepped out.

"*Ja, Fräulein.*"

I was close enough to make out their conversation:

"I'm Erika Wagner. I've come to see my father."

"Did he request your presence?"

"I must see him."

"Did he call for you?"

"No."

"Then you must return home Miss Wagner."

"But…"

"But what, Miss Wagner?"

"I see."

Erika turned away from the door and got back in the Mercedes. I was still scrunched down in the back seat. I watched the guard close the castle gate door. I whispered to Erika, "What happened? Why didn't you insist?"

"I don't know."

"Were you afraid?"

"No."

"Then you must go back. Insist you see your father. Tell the guard it's important."

"I can't. They won't let me in."

"Stay here, and wait for me," I said as I jumped out of the car and ran back down the hill.

It wasn't long before I returned, driving the plumbing truck we had passed earlier. I wore the plumber's white uniform—the previous wearer was tied to a tree beside the road. I drove up to the outer gatehouse, but Erika and the Mercedes were no longer there. I rang the outer gate bell.

"Yes?"

"Royal Flush Plumbing. It's better to have a royal flush than a full house. At your service, sir. I'm here to fix the sewer."

"Our sewer's fine."

"I got a work order says 'sewer line backup' and 'sides you're due a routine inspection of the water-on-demand heaters."

"They're fine."

"That's 'cause we do routine inspections. We never sit down on the job, if you get my drift."

"Not without the bosses oka…"

"We have to do the inspections to guarantee our work."

"I don't think…"

"We're running a might behind. Been a heap o' problems lately, especially in these old castles."

"You are American aren't you?"

"Uh, yes. Germany has a labor shortage."

"I've heard of that. Well, come on then if…"

"It won't take long; I'll be out of here in two shakes."

The big doors began to open—operated by a pulley system—and I drove into the middle ward. Several cars were parked there. Wagner's green Mercedes was there, but Erika wasn't. And next to the Mercedes was the red Citroën, so Dominique was here too.

A tall, beefy, but well-dressed guard stepped out of the inner gatehouse door as I hopped out of the van with a flashlight. I slung a sewer snake over my shoulder.

"Where did you say this backup was?"

I'd hoped he'd forgotten about that. "Well, I won't know that until I run some tests. Just lead me to the lowest floor first."

"Certainly, sir."

Well-trained guard, I thought. I had him, I was in. I couldn't help but thinking: was this guard an android? I stared into his eyes, tried to detect something odd there. I looked for unevenness in his skin texture, I looked for unnatural body movements, but didn't detect anything. If he was an android, he was perfect. Either way, he could kill, and I was closer to him—or it—than I wanted to be.

The guard pointed me to a series of steps that led down to a cellar door.

Stepping down a few mildewed stone steps, I found a door

that creaked open into a low-ceilinged, windowless, dark and musty room. I shone my flashlight. Rats scurried about. The big guard left me there; he was going no further; he was no android. I found my way down a narrow rock-walled passageway. Those people of the Dark-Ages liked tunnels and chambers and winding stairs and tiny windows—very few tiny windows. I don't guess it was their choice, castles were built for defense out of stone and rubble, walls twenty or more feet thick that left only limited space for rooms. I found myself in one of these small rooms, this one with a deep well that must have been the source of the castle's water when it was under siege, but I heard a loud rumbling noise way down in the well. It sounded like rushing water. I looked around for a flashlight—or torch, but didn't find anything I could use.

I climbed a narrow stairway to a room full of television monitors—closed circuit TV—with images of familiar hallways and lab rooms in the castle, and images of rooms in Wagner's mansion: the drawing room, the bedroom, the shower stall. My God, it was Fouquet who had been watching us. But why? I felt dirty. I turned to a large interior window, an unusual thing to find in a castle. Through the window, on a floor below me, was a sterile looking, white laboratory full of electronic equipment. And there was Dr. Montford Fouquet working with several lab technicians around an operating table. On the table lay a detached human hand. A tech touched the hand with an electrode, it twitched and looked down-right freaky.

A door to the lab opened and something under a white sheet was rolled into the room. The sheet was pulled off, revealing a naked torso with legs; it had no arms or head. It looked human enough, but I knew this had to be a machine. I was looking at an assembly plant for androids.

I watched as they attached the hand to the arm—plugging together a few cables, tightening a few nuts, and using what looked much like a soldering iron, to seal the wrist until no joint was apparent. The arms, in similar fashion, were attached to the shoulders. The man—the android—began to look complete except for the head. It reminded me of the headless horseman of *Sleepy Hollow* as he raced along the road with his head in his hands. Actually, in the story, he had been playing a trick on the schoolmaster, Ichabod Crane: he was just carrying a pumpkin under his arms.

A small table was wheeled in next, covered with a sheet under which was a pumpkin—or rather the head; it had to be the head! They placed it beside the android body and pulled off the sheet. I gasped. It was a human-looking head but with no hair; the top of the head was gone, nothing above where the hairline would normally be. There was an open chamber in his skull: the brain was missing. I felt like I was looking at some anatomical prop for studying the human anatomy. But this thing, the body, I doubted it if it had a stomach or spleen or heart—or soul—to study.

A technician in a blue lab coat entered from another room, holding high on a silver platter, a beautiful, mesmerizing piece of machinery about six inches in diameter. Encased in a clear plastic-like substance was a mass of transistors, diodes, and silicon chips. The "neural pathways" seemed to be molded directly into the plastic substance. No wires, no cables. It had to be the Electroplasmic Brain Professor Wagner talked about on his audiotapes.

The technicians inserted the brain into the skull cavity, made several connections, and screwed on the top of the head. They then carefully attached a hairpiece with even more care than they used to insert the brain. At that point, I realized it was the face of the man running for Chancellor of Germany, Helmut Schmidt, the man I had just seen at a rally in front of the police station. Oh God, what were they up to?

My mind went back to Erika; she was somewhere in the

castle. Did the guard take her to her father? Was she safe? I didn't know and I was feeling awfully stupid and helpless.

I left the observation room and continued down a winding flight of stairs and slipped along a narrow passageway. I came upon a larger corridor—

My heart pounded in my throat as I approached a row of rectangular-shaped glass containers about two-and-half-feet square and seven feet tall. The hall was lined with them, container after container, and in these vessels, suspended in a clear, slightly greenish fluid were naked human beings—no, they were androids, I said to myself—they *had* to be androids. They had the human anatomy of both men and woman—beautifully crafted men and women—but their eyes spooked me. They were open, staring straight ahead, an unnerving stare that made me wonder, were they alive? Were they aware of my presence? Could they be watching me? My skin crawled, my stomach felt queasy.

Suddenly, I heard a gunshot and the vessel in front of me shattered into hundreds of pieces. A slimy jelly-like fluid flowed out and then the horrifying thing fell toward me. I reached out trying to stop it from hitting me, but my hands sank into the soft pliable mush until they hit a porous plastic-like skeletal structure. Another shot rang out. An approaching guard was shooting at me. I whirled and ran down the hall.

I ducked into a darkened room and frantically held the door shut. The guard ran past me and on down the hall. I turned on the light to see where I was: a culture room with rows and rows of large petridishes lined along several tables. Over them were hung green-colored fluorescent tubes. Something was being cultivated in those dishes, maybe living skin tissue. Along one black-granite lab table were several rows of plastic trays full of slimy looking things staring up at me; they were eyeballs. As the door behind me banged open, I found another way out of the room. I ran through a chemistry lab full of test tubes and Bunsen burners and then hurried through what looked like a Salvation Army store with its racks of clothes and shoes and coats.

I found myself back in a hallway that looked familiar. I opened one of the double doors and found I was in the auditorium where I first saw Professor Wagner. And down in front, he was still there chalking something on the blackboard. As I approached, Wagner turned and eyed me.

"It's you, Mr. Noble. Nice to see you again. You've got a limp. You didn't hurt yourself on the way down did you?"

"We must get out of here!" I yelled with new found intensity.

"Why?"

"Why! They're after us!"

"You maybe."

"Me? Why?"

"It's okay son, would you sit down please."

"What is this all about?"

"I'll tell you. Sit down."

"What were you four scientists doing at Sunstone?" I asked. "What kind of project were you working on?"

"I'm happy to tell you. We had prototypes, the Sunstone prototypes, wonderful specimens that would surely begin a revolution in way that would change lives forever. We developed androids to serve as much needed slave labor, but without the possibility of backlash, you see, no Muslim revolution, no rioting in streets. You couldn't harm the dignity of these androids; not programmed for that. They would be perfectly happy in their appointed duties. Androids would free the German working class; eliminate the drudgery of their everyday lives. Electric stoves and refrigerators and window air-conditioners revolutionized the homes of the middle class, but it takes a long time for technology to reach the unwashed scratching to make living. With these androids, everyone would have maids, handymen, mechanics, dishwashers—I hate washing dishes.”

“I’m not sure I’m following you, Professor.”

“The poor know how to fix things, they got two hands. They have no choice but to be self-reliant so they can take care of themselves. It’s the upper-middle class that can’t do a damn thing.”

“I’m confused. Who you trying to help? The poor or the middle class or really the…”

“The poor will eventually get access to these new work-saving devices, they always have in the past. Mass production and miniaturization will bring price within everyone’s reach.”

“I’ve heard that one before.”

“You’ve got a refrigerator and television don’t you?”

“And indoor plumbing, yes, but some people still don’t…”

“Son, you take your hot shower for granted.No longer do you need to refill a cistern on your roof; the simple water-heater, that’s all it took for a revolution. Technology has become integrated flawlessly into our society to the point where we can never go back…”

“To outhouses?”

“That’s right.”

“And look, everyone needs medical care. That would be nice would it not, personal doctors, one for each of us? We could program the knowledge and skills needed for diagnosis into any one of our android classes. Doctors are beginning to make less and less house calls. Now just think of it, Mr. Noble, we can each have one of our own…”

“Doctors?”

“Sure, they could diagnose…”

“Could they perform surgery?”

“Well no—but maybe someday. Already many surgical procedures are becoming automated. Even cutting open the body is giving way to less invasive procedures.”

"But these androids…"

"They would solve lot of problems. Androids couldn't hate, wouldn't have fears—at least not fears we hadn't programmed them for—just the ones needed for their everyday survival. They would be immune to disease, free from unhealthy emotions, the android would free man to enjoy life."

"I can't believe you're saying this, Professor. Free from disease maybe, but unhealthy emotions, what's wrong with that? Having a few people with problems, isn't that better than a lot of people with no emotions?"

"Mr. Noble, don't get carried away. These are just the androids; I don't want to replace mankind. Good God no! Imagination, uniqueness, creativity, the ability to dream—without those, mankind would stagnate."

"Okay, okay. Let me get this straight. Androids as assistants, helpers, plumbers—wouldn't that take jobs away from the rest of us?"

"You'd like to be plumber would you"—he looked at my shirt—"work for Royal Flush Plumbing, carry snake all day through sewers? I no think so. And then the jobs that lead to corruption and sicken society, cause drug use and violence, they'd be eliminated, and there would be no more filthy whores on street. No more men playing around behind their wive's backs."

"You've slipped off your cracker, Professor!"

"Have I?"

"What does Dr. Fouquet have to say about this insanity?"

"He, well, he has his own agenda. We had little disagreement…"

"A disagreement that got Stewart and Stravinsky killed?"

"Fouquet's doing."

"Who blew up Sunstone?"

"The company didn't like the direction we were taking our research. The four of us left and covered our tracks."

"The four of you, you did it together then?"

Wagner said nothing.

"Who's the leader of this Frankensteinian band of nut house escapees?"

"Why whatever do you mean, Mr. Noble?"

"This monstrous laboratory!"

"Monstrous, Mr. Noble?"

"In this god-forsaken castle, and back in Fouquet's basement, those ugly, deformed creatures."

"Sorry you saw those, our early experiments…"

"God help us!"

"They're not human. No consciousness, no pain or pleasure, no emotions, not really. Just several levels of circuitry. Consciousness is an illusion, Mr. Noble, and like the wind, you can't see it. What you see are the effects of it. Just programmed responses. The illusion of self—I feel, therefore I am. Free will is an illusion, Mr. Noble. You didn't think *you* had any, did you? Our androids have no conviction of volition and feel no responsibility for what they do."

"Conviction of what? I take responsibility, I know when I'm the cause of something I've done. I know I shot *Fraülein* Detrich; it didn't just happen."

"That's what makes you human and androids just machines—they're like vacuum cleaners, no more than that."

"Then you were never really kidnapped?"

"I was, but it was just Montford getting carried away. He thought I'd no longer work with him, that we had gone our separate ways. But he needed me and I needed him. Someone must have seen Montford's men, thought I was being taken away against my will."

"The press reported it as a kidnapping."

"Unfortunate. Very unfortunate. A rush to be first leads to speculation, to outright falsehoods. You know that, Mr. Noble, you're a newspaper man."

"Well, no, actually, I'm not…"

"Free as a bird, that's what you are…if you choose to be."

"You helped me escape?"

"At that time you *were* in danger, Mr. Noble, from Dr. Fouquet. He wanted you gone, said you were getting too close. I only wanted you as…you're very good looking, Mr. Noble."

"I'm good looking? Christ! What are you talking about? You say I was in danger of my life, but you weren't?"

"Oh, heavens, no…"

"I don't get it. I don't friggin' get it!"

"He just wanted me to help him with problem."

"The black boxes?"

"That's true, our prototypes had to be recharged everyday—a power cell problem.

"Fouquet wanted help with the black boxes?"

"The black boxes, no. We solved that problem some time ago. Those are AC-DC converters, energy cell chargers. A six-hour charge was required while they slept. Don't need those anymore."

"Then the equation, the burnt piece of computer paper?"

"Eating son, eating; our androids can't eat, can't digest food. They don't need the nutrition, of course, and don't need the bulk to dispose of. No, it's about the illusion, the illusion of eating. They must appear like humans in every possible way in order to defy detection."

"The equation addressed that problem?"

"No. Actually it's mechanism by which our androids can taste food electronically, respond to chemicals as a flavor."

"Taste buds?"

"In a way. Androids can't actually feel anything as we do, no nerve endings. They're actually just programmed responses to external inputs. Now we're working on way to…"

"Can they drink?"

"Sure, but in limited quantities."

"Can they bleed if they cut their finger? Bruise if they're hit..."

Suddenly, the auditorium door crashed open and two guards came running after me. I ran out the side door and down yet another hall.

What was going on? Wagner was off his rocker. Doctors in every home. Fearless robotic plumbers. The man had been spending too much time in his laboratory. Maybe I'd been chasing after the wrong bad guy. I didn't actually know what Fouquet was up to. Maybe he was the one in the right, the ethical, moral one—if *anyone* around here was. What was I getting close to? The androids weren't the whole story.

thirty nine

I OPENED a large door into the castle's Great Hall. The enormous room was spanned by a timber-trussed roof with wooden stairways winding to doorways at several levels. The smoke from fires used to heat the Great Hall back in the Middle Ages blackened the beams, and on the walls were tapestries, paintings, and shields with coats of arms. The room contained the huge computer main frame I had been looking for with its flashing lights and spinning tape reels. I could see a few keypunch machines used to punch little rectangular holes in IBM cards so that the lines of code could be read into the computer. And magnetic tape disk drives jumped forward and then quickly reversed themselves automatically as they searched for data. Printing machines jerked out reams of paper that stacked itself in a wire bin. This computer would take a lot of electricity, and it now hit me: the boiler room I crossed over the first time I was here had to be an electric generator. They weren't getting electricity from the city, they were generating it themselves: steam-powered generators using coal—or maybe from a diverted river flowing under the castle—

Suddenly, a computer technician turned toward me and looked at me as if I was a vile computer bug. He came at me; I grabbed a huge roll of magnetic tape and threw it at him. Then I took a lance hanging on the wall and braced the back end against the wall behind me. The tech leaped at me—the rod slid through his body—he crackled, shook violently, and began to smoke. Sparks flew as he fell into the wall. At least androids weren't indestructible.

From out of the corner of my eye, I saw Dr. Fouquet high up on a catwalk that wound its way through the roof trusses. He stood there like an overseer, watching from afar, letting his androids do his dirty work. When our eyes met, his glare burned at mine. He casually turned away as if I wasn't worth his time. I raced toward the wooden staircase and made my way to the rafters. I raced along the high catwalk, the computer equipment appearing far down below me like so much dollhouse furniture. Fouquet took another set of steps that turned back in my direction, but which now placed him across from me, across a wide chasm between truss cords. I grabbed an overhead beam and swung out over the opening and dropped in front of Fouquet. He stopped, surprised.

"Mr. Noble!"

"Why are you trying to kill me?" I asked.

"I'm not, Mr. Noble. Though I admit, I did want to get rid of you originally, but Professor Wagner saw you could be useful. He assure me you were harmless, but you were getting the police to sniffing around like little curious roaches, and I not like that. But Wagner want you, and you were so much fun, Noble, letting your willie lead you around like that. We decide we could make use of your talents—in our testing—and you performed beautifully, Mr. Noble."

"What are you saying?"

"You're a pawn, Noble. You've been led around on a leash and didn't even know it. Don't you get it? Move aside, Noble."

"You can't be allowed to contin…"

Fouquet reached for my throat with both hands. I pushed them away with my forearms.

"You're nothing but trouble, Noble. You're destroying my dreams for a better world."

"They're *your* dreams, not mine."

"I can bring peace to the world. Can't you see that? No more wars or petty squabbles over land or money. There'd be no more hate and bigotry, no fear and suspicion. They could all get along. Perfect human beings, without personal problems. They wouldn't get sick. They wouldn't require large plots of land to raise food. They wouldn't ask for divorce, they would, simply, do as they were told."

"You're off your friggin' rocker."

"I'm Lord of Rheinstein, this is *my* domain."

"You're the Lord of an Evil Hell and your reign is about to come to an end. I'm going to see to that."

"You can't stop me now. Don't you see, I must finish my work."

I reached for him.

"Stop! Lay your hands off me. I must expand my factories, I have to make plans, I must perfect."

"Perfect! I've heard that word entirely too much. There's no such thing—perfection. I saw your 'Helmut Schmidt' re-creation. You plan to place android doubles in high political positions, don't you? You plan to get more and more of them in office until you control the entire world."

"It's the only way," replied Fouquet. "Only one man can save the world from its insanity. I can make things happen, get things done, no bickering of political parties, no fickle public easily swayed by emotion instead of good common sense."

"So, you want just one government?"

"What does it matter really. What do governments do? They control your life now under the guise of National security—for your own good they say. And they take most of your hard-earned money. But there'll be no need for that if there's just one world government…take your hands off me."

Fouquet tried to push me aside—I was pushed off balance, my hand grabbed for the railing as he passed by me.

I turned, "Fouquet!"

"Rot in hell, Noble!"

I rushed toward him and pushed him down to the catwalk floor.

"I was wrong; I should have killed you."

We throttled each other's throat and rolled left and then right; Fouquet's strained face was full of hate and vengeance. He tried to get his knee to my groin, but, thank the Lord, he was off center, hitting my thigh instead. We struggled on and my heart pounded, my face flushed, blood coursing through my veins at a gallop. Fouquet grabbed for the railing trying to wrench himself from my grip, but his foot slid and he slipped under the railing, his body now dangling thirty feet above the computer floor. One hand on the railing kept him from falling to his death. I grabbed his other arm and held on. Way down below, I saw Professor Wagner and Erika enter the Great Hall. She was here; she was safe. They looked up at the commotion on the catwalk. My eyes locked on Erika's. I wanted to cry out. I wanted to say I was sorry. I wanted to say please forgive me.

Erika seemed to show some concern, real emotion for the first time.

She cried out, "NOBLE!"

I love her; I know it. A decision I made of my own free will. I pulled harder on Fouquet's arm and was able to get his other hand to the railing. I reached down for a leg and lifted, but the weight was too much for me: Fouquet twisted in panic, pulling me forward. I fell head over heals, my hands reaching, reaching, reaching for something—anything. I had made my last mistake. Over I went. I wasn't who I thought I was. I wasn't ready for love. I didn't have the confidence to take on life's realities; I had no bullets in my gun. I saw a glimpse of Erika paralyzed in horror—disbelief on her innocent child-like face—as I tumbled through the air, my hands reaching and finding only air.

Erika's face would be burned forever into my memory.

forty

Erika ran over to Noble and kneeled down. His body was contorted—hips, legs and ankles twisted well beyond their normal range of motion. She ran her hands softly across Noble's hand and watched him gasping for air. His eyelids suddenly slid open and fixed eyes stared skyward. A single teardrop welled up in one of Erika's eyes and ran slowly down her cheek.

Erika looked up to the rafters to see two technicians pulling Dr. Fouquet safely onto the catwalk. Professor Wagner pulled on Erika's arm. "Come, we must go."

Erika stood there weakly and looked to her father for answers—and found none. Another tear ran from her eyes. "I love him," she said.

"That's good my dear."

"I love him."

"I'm sorry Erika. Come with me."

Just as they started to leave the computer room, Dr. Fouquet entered with the two technicians at his side. "Gentleman, we must rerun program Sixteen Zebra. Reset the tape drives, please." Fouquet passed Erika and Professor Wagner and approached a computer console. He grabbed a stack of IBM punch cards, wrapped a rubber band around them, and dropped them into a cardboard box stacked full of still more cards.

"Dr. Fouquet!" said Erika sternly.

Fouquet turned toward her, "Yes, my dear?"

Fouquet froze. Erika had a tin pistol in her hand: *The Liberator*, the one Noble found at her house. She pointed it straight at Fouquet and looked at him with the face of a pretty maiden who had been horribly wronged, and with all her heart said, "I loved him. He was *my* knight."

Without hesitation, Erika pulled the trigger.

Fouquet could see the bullet exploding from the muzzle. He knew the end was near. The bullet penetrated his belly, went cleanly through his body, and hit the console behind him. The console shorted out and sparks spewed forth. Blood oozed from Fouquet's mouth and he slowly toppled to the floor; a surprised look fixed forever on his wretched face. Professor Wagner stood frozen, stunned with surprise, his partner and friend laying dead to the world, and then—

"Erika! You bitch!" sounded a wail from afar.

Erika turned to see Dominique approaching with fiery determination.

"You evil bitch!" repeated Dominique as Professor Wagner tried to hold her back.

"You did this, it's your fault."

Wagner interceded, "Girls! We must be civil, we taught you to be dignified ladies."

Dominique pushed the doctor aside with ruthless abandon. "He was mine!"

Dominique grabbed Erika. Erika dropped the smoking gun, it clattered to the floor.

"I loved him," replied Erika as she tried to push Dominique away, but Dominique—with her long, manicured fingernails—ripped four furrowed gashes into Erika's face. Erika grabbed Dominique's jet-black hair by the nape and pulled hard, wrenching Dominique's neck backward. Erika pulled further, twisting Dominique around and onto the floor. The black-haired beauty wrapped her long legs around Erika's waist like a vice and squeezed with everything she had. Erika struggled to free herself. Dominique reached for the pistol, but it lay just beyond her fingertips. She screamed in frustration, "Get off me bitch!"

Erika replied, "Where did you learn such words, sister? Father didn't teach you."

"Shit, I know fuck too and fornicator, and you're a fornicating whore," screamed Dominique and then spat in Erika's face. Erika grimaced and welled up with a nauseous loathing.

Erika leaned toward Dominique and took a big healthy bite out of her rosy red cheek and spit it back into Dominique's face. Dominique clawed at Erika's clothes with raw hatred, ripping them to shreds. Wagner tried to pull the two fighting hens apart. Erika got to her feet, her cheek bleeding, her hair and clothes in disarray, pieces of her expensive finery—and her charm—dragging on the floor. Her feet pigeon-toed and her knees bowed inward, the long-legged beauty looked comical as she brushed her auburn hair back from her face.

Dominique then hauled herself to her feet. Her burgundy lipstick now looked the color of dried blood.

"Look what you've done to yourselves!" barked Wagner in astonishment at the raw brutality he had just witnessed.

Dominique fumed with rage and lunged forward and pushed Erika into the console. Dominique fell forward on top of her, sparks flew, and the already smoking console, flared up in flames. Erika got her hands around Dominique's neck and squeezed with all her life-giving might. Erika's back smoldered and sizzled. Dominique's hands fell to the console as she tried to brace herself, and when she tried to pull free, wires shorted out, and the heavens thundered. The Professor was forced to step back. The skin of Dominique and Erika began to flow off their skeletons. Their faces losing all form—high cheekbones, beautiful white teeth, delicate eyebrows and luscious lips—dissolving into nothingness. Melting plastic goo ran off the top of the console and dripped onto the floor in little flaming gobs of goo.

Professor Wagner stood there, motionless. Not surprised, not horrified, but looking as if there had been a great loss. He stared at the Sunstone prototypes, the most perfect G-Class models ever produced.

Professor Wagner took the box of IBM punch cards and headed for the door of the putrid, smoke-filled room. He stepped around the twisted body of Brandon Noble, past the body of Montford Fouquet, and left the Great Hall. He made his way quietly down the long brightly-lit corridor.

The double doors in front of him swung open. Wagner's eyes bugged out of his head and he dropped the box and stacks of cards slid across the floor.

There, standing in the doorway was Dr. Montford Fouquet.

"Montford! I'm so relieved."

"As you should be, Professor."

"I thought that was you—"

"I'm well my friend, Erika just shot my android duplicate."

"The new one you've been working on?"

"Yes."

"It had me fooled. Great work, Montford. He didn't throw sparks and burn up."

"I find way to ground him in the big toe. He actually blew a fuse instead of himself."

"Bravo. And I thought I saw some blood coming from his mouth?"

"You did, but long way to go before we can perfect that illusion."

"Shall we go?"

"After you."

The two men left through the double doors, walking down the long, white, nondescript hallway.

"A little melodramatic wasn't it, Doctor?" asked Wagner. "My kidnapping. I would have come to see you voluntarily."

"Sorry, but it was April Fools Day and I thought…"

"You thought stupid; you got the police on our case. They could have exposed our entire operation."

"I didn't know someone would see the goons and report it. But it was fun, wasn't it?"

"And Mr. Noble, he fell right into our lap. Never kiss a horse on the mouth."

"That's 'never look a gift horse in the mouth.' He did make a good research subject, didn't he?"

"It was good idea of yours Wilhelm, I was going to kill him."

"You didn't have to turn loose your imbecilic hired hands on him."

"That started with that ingrate Stuart who was going to tell all; I just wanted them to rough him up a bit…"

"And it spun out of control like an aeroplane without ailerons—and then Branko took Erika for his own pleasure."

"Can't blame him, can you?"

"So which was the better G-class prototype, yours or…"

"I think Noble liked yours better," said Fouquet.

"They were good, weren't they, Doctor?"

"Our G-class models, they'll make good *Geliebte*, good mistresses."

"They're wonderful creatures, satisfy a man to ultimate ecstasy."

"The programming was easy. The orgasmic response, that was easy…"

But testing, field-testing, we've got to work on that. Mr. Noble was not an easy subject to keep up with."

"No."

"A very conflicted man."

"Don't be too hard on him. He was an American. He didn't know his own limitations."

"Ha, you should have seen him skinny down those bed sheets when I told him you were coming after him."

"Caging him in my brank didn't hurt."

"You were serious then."

"Maybe." A glint of mystery flashed across his eyes.

"Well, we've a lot of work to do."

The two men descended the entrance steps to the courtyard and crossed to the gardens of the inner ward.

"I'm not sure how we're going to reign in their unrestrained sexual urges," said Dr. Montford Fouquet.

"Maybe realign the CV-gyro to work like a governor of sorts."

"The reasoning subroutines need a rewrite."

"Possibly."

"And Wilhelm, you've got to program your G-class girls with more socializing babble, that Lorelei tale of yours, and all those Bacharach song lyrics, just because you were born there, frankly…"

"I like Bacharach…Oh, Montford, did you notice: I think the girls showed signs of jealously?"

"You mean their fight over Noble?"

"Well, I'm not sure that was the motivation for that little tiff."

"No? Maybe not."

"And Erika, you know what she said to me?"

"No, Wilhelm, what?"
"She said, 'I love him'."
"Splendid, that's splendid."
Wagner and Fouquet passed through the defense tower and over the drawbridge. They got into the emerald-green Mercedes and waved to the guard as they drove past the cherry-red Citroën and through the outer-ward gatehouse. Two knights in full armor stood guard at the entrance.

epilogue

Brandon Noble actually survived the fall from the catwalk, but was paralyzed from the neck down. He also contracted a bad case of poison ivy on his hands—that he also managed to transfer to his "pretty" face. Helmut Schmidt became the Chancellor of Germany in January of 1974, and Inspector Gerhard Schultz recovered fully from his wounds, but died two years later in a gun battle with what he called "The Plastic People."

What happened in the spring of '73 is true and if you still don't believe Brandon Noble, the Berlin National Archives holds a brown envelope with the telling words "ERIKA" scrawled across it along with a 36-exposure roll of film that was found in his Nikon camera.

And remember this: Look around you. Look carefully. How do you know that the people you meet on the sidewalk are not computers programmed to simulate people? How, for the love of God, do you know *you're* not?

Das Ist Alles

DMO1-2002-V5